STUPID

STUPID

KIM FIRMSTON

James Lorimer & Company Ltd., Publishers
Toronto

James Lorimer & Company Ltd., Publishers acknowledges the support of the Ontario Arts Council. We acknowledge the financial support of the Government of Canada through the Canada Book Fund for our publishing activities. We acknowledge the support of the Canada Council for the Arts which last year invested $24.3 million in writing and publishing throughout Canada. We acknowledge the Government of Ontario through the Ontario Media Development Corporation's Ontario Book Initiative.

Cover design: Meghan Collins
Cover image: Shutterstock

Library and Archives Canada Cataloguing in Publication

Firmston, Kim, author
        Stupid / Kim Firmston.

(SideStreets)
Issued in print and electronic formats.
ISBN 978-1-4594-0612-4 (bound).--ISBN 978-1-4594-0611-7 (pbk.).--ISBN 978-1-4594-0613-1 (epub)

        I. Title. II. Series: SideStreets

PS8611.I75S88 2014   jC813'.6   C2013-907270-5
C2013-907271-3

James Lorimer & Company Ltd.,   Distributed in the United States by:
Publishers   Orca Book Publishers
317 Adelaide Street West, Suite 1002   P.O. Box 468
Toronto, ON, Canada   Custer, WA, USA
M5V 1P9   98240-0468
www.lorimer.ca

Printed and bound in Canada
Manufactured by Webcom in Toronto, Ontario in March 2014.
Job #411695

*Dedicated to the amazing and awesome
parkour community of Calgary.*

1

LEAPING SHADOWS

Stupid.

Maybe I am stupid.

Stupid for doing this.

In front of me, a sharp white floodlight throws hard shadows against a grey brick wall. Above me, cobalt-blue twilight fades quickly into the dimness of night. I pull my camera out of its travel bag, check the focus, snap a photo, then switch over to video. The old brewery is silent. Dead silent. Graveyard silent. That's good. It means I'm still in the clear. I shoot some footage of the chain-link fence. Its entwined metal casts lace-like shadows on the broken concrete. The rusted barbwire, partially collapsed at its top, hums in the warm spring breeze. I can see a tetanus shot in my future if I try to break in that way.

I switch off the camera, snap the lens cap back on, and sneak, crouched and guilty, down a private road parallel to the backside of the brewery. The gate that normally closes this off is open and welcoming. The *Private Property* sign, not so much. There's no way to claim innocence if I get caught. I mean, it's not like I could miss that sign. Still, I wasn't the one who left the gate open. On my right-hand side I look for a break in the fence — some way of squeezing in or under. Twenty feet in I see a spot where the wire is bent up off the ground enough for a small coyote to squeeze under. Or me, if I don't breathe.

Lying down, back scraping the dirt, I hold my camera tight. My camera's safety is everything. Me, I can get scratched, bloody, mangled. My camera? Never. It's worth gold. I don't let go of it for a second, even when the fence rubs against my nose, reeking of old metal and dog piss.

Finally I'm through, kicking the last of my body into the forbidden zone. Ice crystals work their way into the neck of my sweater, making me shiver. I hope I was quiet enough. I did try to keep the grunting and chain rattling to a bare minimum.

I'm really not sure where the security guard is. I saw him pass on the other side of the building before I attempted all this, but I don't know how long it will be before he comes to this side. If at all. It *is* full of saplings and weeds pushing up through cracks in the concrete. All my skulking could be for nothing.

I roll to my feet and press my back against the grey brick wall, like I'm in a spy movie. Looking up, I search for cameras. The storage company that owns this property has them all over. I'm hoping my black top and navy cargo pants will keep anyone from spotting me. Blond hair is no help in situations like this. I yank up my hood. So far, so good.

I hear a crack and a thump. It's distant. I try to picture where it's coming from. Above? Maybe from farther in the yard? I wonder if it's the guard heading my way. I hold still, listening, but there are no more sounds, except the usual traffic off of Ninth Avenue and a train approaching, its wheels singing as it heads for Alyth yard. Using the train noise as a cover, I creep slowly, carefully, along the building, taking the lens cap off my camera as I go.

I try to picture this place a hundred years ago, when it was the Calgary Brewing and Malting Company. Back then it was a hopping place. The hub of the community. People brought their families to have picnics and look at the fish swimming in artesian well water. Now the park is locked up. The aquarium long gone. Even the bison statue has been fenced in, its butt tagged with some Stampede ad.

Most of the place is falling apart — the brew house, the racking room, though the big, red-brick chimney still sticks out of the ground like a tower in a medieval castle. The storage company fixed up the main building. A place for hoarders to put their stuff. They even had one of those storage war auction things last month, like the people on TV. The place probably has some valuables, which would explain the security.

Yeah, I'm being really stupid.

If you ask my dad, it's not a surprise. He seems to think if I'm not studying or doing some kind of sport, I'm wasting my life. Moviemaking is not a waste; it's art. But getting him to understand that is like trying to film a rock concert with a macro lens. No point.

Keeping low, I creep along until I'm by the chimney. It's immense, poking the night sky way above me. There's a tower nearby, all grey ladders and rusted metal coming apart at the joints. I head over and tentatively test a step low to the ground. It creaks and groans. I'll die if I climb that. Instead, I move down a narrow passage lost to time. There's a lot of garbage in here, some of it maybe dating back to the early days of the brewery. It casts hard shadows, making the cracked concrete look evil. Like a demon will claw its way out from the depths below. Crumpled paper rustles past, making my skin shiver and itch with sudden fright. I grip the camera, check my settings, zoom in. An old tire becomes ominous in the gloom, like an eye. I focus in on that. A big, rubber monster eye looking into my soul. I shoot the buildings farther on. Deep in the maze of shadows where everything goes black. Pure black. And that's why I *had* to come here. This place is perfect. It's dark. Crumbling. Disorganized. Garbage.

Like me.

I've been trying not to buy into the label for years. Stupid. But when everyone calls you that, it gets kind of hard to keep denying it. *How can I push away the word when every test I write barely crawls above a fifty per cent? When red scrawls of pen remind me to make an effort, work harder, listen in class — and that's all I've been doing?* Obviously they must be right. I'm being stupid by denying it. It's just taken me this long to finally come to terms with all that.

Except, I don't really want to.

I catch a flicker of light reflecting off the camera screen. Spin. Drop behind an upended wooden palette. Snap the camera off in mid shot. It makes a click. I wince. Scanning, I can't see anything. No flashlight, no guard, nothing. Maybe it was something else. Still, I wait. Back pressed hard against the dusty brick wall. Finally I turn the camera on again. Continue my journey deeper, looking for that perfect shot.

There's an opening ahead. A bit of courtyard, I guess. Broken bricks litter the ground. Old wood, too, maybe from barrels. The place reeks of rot. Another flash catches my eye. This time it's an old glass pop bottle. I wonder if it's from the days of prohibition. When alcohol was banned and the brewery remade itself, selling soda and aerated water.

I wish I could remake myself that easily.

I stand the bottle up amongst the bricks, letting the harsh white security light glint off its surface. In my camera lens, it looks like a jewel. A diamond sitting on a mound of rubble. I film twenty seconds worth of footage. A lifetime in the world of moviemaking.

Things look different when you view them through a lens. There's a depth you don't get in real life. Small things become huge. Unimportant things can take up the whole screen. And things that are irritating can be blurred or moved out of the shot entirely. My teacher tells me to focus. With my camera I can choose my focus. I can twist the world any way I want.

Mom tries to be helpful, encouraging me when, even she admits, she has no idea how to do my homework. She considers it a stage I'll grow out of. I'm sixteen. I haven't grown out of it. It's not going to happen. Then there's Dad. To him I'm a failure, dumb, stupid. The thirty-two per cent on my social studies test today just proves his point.

If people asked me what I knew, instead of making me write it out, I could tell them. But they don't. It's always essays and tests and *try to make an effort*. Anyway, it doesn't matter. I'm not going to university like everyone wants. As soon as I'm eighteen, I'm taking off for Hollywood and doing what I was born to do. Make movies.

I slink farther into the courtyard, camera aimed high. I'm trying to catch the slivered moon peeking out between black spotted clouds, lighting up the dark brick edge between the sky and the roof, when a shadow flickers. Well, not exactly flickers, more like darts. Which is weird, because shadows aren't supposed to move. Not on their own. The shadow races along the rooftop and leaps, flying through the air, from one squared-off roof section to another. Then it disappears. I can't believe I'm catching this. I scan the landing spot. A loud "HEY!" makes me jump.

The security guard.

I snap my head to look around. I don't spot him, but he sounds close. Too close.

"HEY!" the voice shouts again. "STOP!"

A quick backtrack gets me to a three-foot-wide opening between buildings. I slip in, heart pounding in my ears, fingers shaking. I turn off the camera and snap on the lens cap. I'm not sure if the guard is yelling at me or the shadow on the roof. But whichever it is, it's best to stay out of sight.

I sink down into a crouch. The ancient grey bricks shed mortar like a salt shaker onto my shoulders. I listen hard. My ears like telephoto lenses. I pull my hood back a bit. But there's nothing. No sounds, no more yelling. The image of the shadow running and leaping ploughs through my head. I turn on the camera. Play the footage. It's definitely someone running across the rooftops. But why?

Heavy footsteps crunch concrete, coming my way. A flashlight beam flickers this way and that just beyond my hiding spot. I hold my breath. Above, spotty grey clouds cover the moon. I wonder if I should run for it. There's a clatter of rock against brick. A rustle of fabric. Crumbling wall rains down on me. The sky is blocked from my view. My mouth opens to scream. A hand slaps it shut.

2

STICK

Rust and dirt make me gag as fingers push against my teeth. I fight to pull myself free, clutching my camera and using my elbows. No one is stealing my stuff.

My attacker points urgently into the courtyard. The pale flashlight beam swoops into our hiding spot. I get the message. Nod. My mouth is released. My camera's viewing screen illuminates the front of my hoodie. I clutch it tight to my chest, hoping the fabric will be enough to hide it. I can't turn it off without a sound. And, right now, we don't need any sounds.

Neither one of us breathes.

The guard gets closer. His scowling face and navy blue baseball cap are visible as he leans in. He waves the flashlight up and down. Shines the light farther inside the gap where we are hiding. The edge of the beam brushes my runner. I resist the urge to snatch my foot away. If I don't move I might blend with the rest of the garbage in here. The light stays on my shoe. I fight the trembling that has taken over my body. I want to run. Just bolt my way out and race to safety. It's the hardest thing in the world to stay still.

The guard lets out a grunt. His boots scrape the concrete as he steps even closer. The beam is now millimetres from my leg. I could be found out with a flick of his wrist. My heart pounds. Lips go numb. Tingles trace the bridge of my nose. I've never been this scared in my life. The guard grunts again, then shoots his beam up the wall as he turns away, footsteps receding. I suck in a huge breath.

"Holy crap!" the shadowy figure beside

me whispers. "That was close. Thanks for not blowing my cover."

"Yeah, you too," I reply.

The shadow laughs. "No problem." He stands and jumps, grabbing a jutting brick and climbing the wall like some kind of Spiderman.

"Hang on," I say.

He drops back down as soundlessly as the first time. "What?"

I pull my camera away from my hoodie and play the footage I shot before I was chased into hiding — the shadow leaping from one building to the next. "Is that you?"

"Yeah. Wow! Great shot."

"Thanks." In the light of the camera's screen, I can sort of make out this shadow-guy's face. He seems to be about sixteen, like me, though his skin isn't pasty white like mine, and he looks like he's in better shape. His black hair sticks up everywhere in an overly long crewcut, and one of his promin-ent cheekbones has a streak of orange rust on its tan skin.

"So," the kid says, "you casin' the place? Gonna rob it?"

I look around at the sharp triangle shadows, peeking moonlight glinting off ragged metal, the ominous tower in the distance. "No. Just doing some filming. You?"

"Parkour."

"Parkour?" I've heard of the word before, but I can't quite place it. "What's that?"

The kid runs two fingers up his vertical hand and makes like they're flipping. "Parkour."

I get the picture, I think. "You mean that free running stuff when people zip up walls and fly from roofs and things? Like in that James Bond movie, *Casino Royale*?"

"Yeah, and you recorded one of my better precision jumps."

"Why here, though?"

"Look at the place," the kid says. "It was made for parkour." He waves his arm upward. "It's perfect."

"Except for the guard."

He chuckles. "Yeah, and the collapsing . . . um, everything."

"This place *is* over a hundred years old."

"Really? What a death trap." He offers his hand. "I'm Stick."

"Stick?"

"Because I always stick my landings — you?"

"Martin." I shake his hand. It's strong and rough with calluses and grit.

Our hiding spot brightens with a flashlight beam. "Got you!" the security guard yells.

Stick once more grabs the jutting brick and pulls himself up and onto the low roof of the building we're hiding behind. "Come on!" he calls.

I swing my camera around behind me, the strap putting its entire weight on my throat, cutting my ability to breathe in half. Jumping up, my fingers barely catch the brick Stick grabbed so easily. I try to jam the rubber of my running shoe into a crack and finally struggle onto the spongy roof. The security guard is on his way up too. This terrifies me. And not because I'm afraid of being caught. I don't think the roof can hold three people, but Stick is already moving. He leaps onto a big, black pipe attached to the main building. At one time the pipe might have been a chute for grain; now it's old and rusting and defiantly not stable.

"Come on!" Stick calls again. He swings from the pipe onto a bunch of narrow metal tubes that run horizontally, bolted to the side of the building, moving along them hand over hand like it's nothing.

There's a creak behind me as the roof groans.

The security guard is up.

I run to the gap, ready to jump, but stop short of the edge. Admittedly the jump to the pipe is not a huge distance, but I'll never make it. I'm clumsy and uncoordinated.

"Jump!" Stick shouts. He's already at the end of the tubes, knee swinging onto an aluminum ledge jutting out from the corner of the building.

I go to make the leap again, but chicken out a second time and have to windmill my arms just to keep from tipping over the edge. The guard grunts. I glance back at his ruby face. He's huffing pretty hard and not really moving after the effort of climbing the bricks. And I thought I was out of shape.

I look around. The pipe's my best bet, but . . .

"You can do it," Stick calls encouragingly. He almost looks like he's enjoying this.

"I'll fall!"

"You won't."

The security guard finally begins to lumber over. He's in no rush. It's pretty obvious I'm not going anywhere.

Until he reaches for my camera.

It's still hanging down my back, out of the way of bumps and scrapes. When he snags it, it's like an electric shock hitting every nerve in my body. I yank and . . .

Leap.

Wrap my arms around the pipe. Slip down, shirt catching. Metal scraping my gut. Swing my right hand over to the silver tubes. My camera is strangling me. Makes screaming impossible.

"Hand over hand," Stick advises.

The guard's flashlight makes a white circle around me. Like I'm an escaping prisoner. "I'll get you!" he yells. His voice echoes off the brick and reverberates through the pipe.

I hand over hand it, palms burning, eyes darting at the ground with every move. *I'm not going to make it. I'm not.*

But failure here would really hurt.

I don't even care about the guard by the time I get near Stick. My throat aches. My arms throb. A hangnail I didn't even know about stings. My hood falls down. Stick's hand slaps down, griping my wrist. "Grab the pipes above you with your hand," he orders. "Then swing your leg up."

I kind of get what he's saying. There's another set of black pipes that come down right above me at a diagonal before straightening out closer to the roof. If I can get up to those, I might make it. But I don't think I can. I haven't had a solid breath since I started running. My camera has hit my back so many times I've developed a bruise. My neck is rubbed raw. "I can't," I croak.

Stick scowls, his face dire in the shadows. "You have to."

"I . . ."

"Swing your hand up. I'll pull you. Just like monkey bars in grade two."

I always fell off the monkey bars in grade two. But I swing my hand up while he gives a heave in time with my movements. Grab the fist-thick pipes. Get my knee up on the narrow tubes. Then the tip of my shoe. Stick lets go. The pipes groan and shudder under my weight.

"I'm going to die!" I gasp.

"Keep moving," Stick says, his voice steady.

I glance back. The guard is gone.

"Move along the pipes until they level out," Stick orders. "Then use them like a ladder to climb onto the roof."

The groaning, popping, and shifting of the ever-loosening pipes keep me from arguing. By the time I'm ready to climb up, Stick is already above me. I don't know how he did that.

It takes another bunch of cursing and scrambling before I'm up beside him. This roof isn't much better than the one we came off of. The toe of my shoe breaks through within my first five steps. "I'm going to die."

"Then let's get down."

"Down? We just got up."

Stick runs a couple of steps, then stops and waits while I put my camera into its travel bag. If it comes to a choice between getting caught or my camera getting smashed — I'm turning myself in. Besides, my back has had enough punishment, and I need to breathe. I sling the camera bag so it rides on the back of my hip and has less danger of getting bumped or hit. Stick is darting back and forth. He doesn't say "hurry up," but I can tell that's what he wants. "Come on. The guard is probably heading around the building. Or calling the cops."

That gets me going.

I follow Stick as we race over the wide expanse of rooftop. It looks like Minecraft up here. There are square buildings on top of larger square buildings with ladders linking them together. Brick walls sport large, ragged holes dripping with pigeon crap. The place stinks of rot. I want to hold my breath, but I'm puffing too hard.

We hit wall after wall as we race. Sometimes we're going up. Sometimes down. I use the barely clinging ladders. Stick leaps, rolls, and runs. He has to wait for me more than once. Finally we hit our last cliff — a three-foot drop leading to a slanting aluminum roof followed by another fifteen-foot drop onto a loading dock. There is no ladder.

"I can't," I say, backing up a few steps.

"You can. Follow me."

"I don't do parkour."

Stick flashes me a wild toothy grin. "Anyone can do parkour."

"I'm clumsy."

"Look." Stick's pointing beside the ledge of the old loading dock below. What's left of a frame surrounds it, tarp fabric snapping in the wind. "Slide down the roof and climb down that. I can hold your camera."

I shake my head. No one holds my camera. "It's okay. I can do it."

Stick claps my shoulder. "I'll go down first and spot you. You're going to be fine." He launches himself off the building and slides two footed down the ramp before leaping, spinning his body in a 180-degree turn, grabbing the frame with both hands and swinging onto the platform below. He looks up, grinning. "Come on."

I sit down. Carefully lower my feet onto the angled siding. They slip. *I'm going to die.* "I can't," I call.

"You can," Stick calls back. His eyes dart sideways. There's a bouncing circle of light in the distance.

The security guard.

I push off the roof, land with butt slipping

on the metal, rubber-soled shoes making poor brakes. My feet slide over the edge before I can get anywhere near to a stop. I roll on my belly to halt my momentum, camera banging. I wince, and not because my thigh scrapes the edge of the metal, and my fingers smash the rusting frame in a panicked attempt to find safety.

The metal barely has time to complain before I'm down beside Stick and leaping off the loading dock onto the concrete.

"I see you!" the guard yells, almost caught up. "I can ID you!"

The train crossing, a quarter of a block away, starts dinging. Flashing yellow lights shine brightly in the night, alternating on the big, wooden Xs. Stick grabs my arm and yanks me toward it. Thirty feet down the track, the locomotive's headlights are blinding. Stick doesn't stop. He drags me past the barriers and right onto the track, the train bearing down on us.

In the push of air pressure coming off the

engine I can't hear the shriek of the breaks, the howling of the horn, or even my own screams. All noises become static as we leap to safety, the train blasting by inches from our backs. Us on one side — the guard on the other.

"Keep moving," Stick says. He gives me another tug, taking off at an escape pace.

By the time we hit Starbucks, a good five blocks away, my legs are Jell-O. My side is cramped and burning. My throat, dry from huffing, sticks to itself and makes it impossible to swallow. I go in and buy two overpriced waters and hand one to Stick as we sink to the curb outside the door and down them in one go.

"See, you *can* do parkour," Stick says, wiping spilled water from his tan face.

"It was luck," I say. "That's all. Blind luck."

Stick laughs, pushing his fingers through his black hair. "Yeah. Maybe. Your camera okay?"

I take it out and give it a once-over, checking through the last bit of footage. "It's fine."

Stick shakes his head. "I still can't believe that shot you got of me. You're good. You on Facebook?" I nod. He pulls out his phone and sends me a friend request right there.

"You should join us at the park. We could teach you some basic parkour stuff. You might like it."

I shake my head. "Naw. I'm more into film."

"Then," Stick says, "You could film us."

I nod. "Yeah. That would be fun."

"Great. I'll let you know when we're meeting up." He stands and stretches. "I better get home. Nice meeting you, Martin." Stick shakes my hand again, then sets off at a run, leaping over a bench that gets in his way.

I limp toward home too. My palms on fire and legs complaining about the sudden physical activity. Really, I want to rest more. Maybe have a coffee or two. But I have lots of footage to go through, and I know if I stay out any longer, Dad is going to flip.

If he hasn't already.

3

TIME TO ACT!

The door to the house creaks. I wince and tip-toe in.

"Martin, is that you?" Dad booms. He's in the living room, watching the Stanley Cup playoffs.

"Yeah, Dad, I'm home." I swing my camera from my hip closer to my back and hope he'll zoom in on my face or at least keep panning toward the TV. I also dust the remaining dirt from my knees and butt. I don't need questions. Questions lead to discussions and discussions lead to yelling — especially since Pierce.

Four months ago, back in January, when the company my Dad works for was taken over and reorganized, Dad got a new boss. Harry Jefferson. Mr. Jefferson is nuts about his sixteen-year-old athletic, genius son, Pierce. He boasts daily about Perfect Pierce, *the amazing boy*. My dad gets to see pictures of Pierce in his hockey uniform with the big captain's C on his chest. He gets handed Pierce's provincial soccer trophies and is shown Pierce's framed honours-with-distinction certificates from his first semester of grade ten.

To say Dad is competitive would be like saying water is wet. Dad tries to compensate for his lack of a decent male heir by hyping my little sister, Carly. But it's not the same, and he knows it. Especially when Mr. Jefferson asks how I'm doing.

"You're late," Dad grumbles, ambling over.

I look at my phone. I am, by half an hour. "Sorry, I lost track of time."

"Breathe on me," Dad sticks his nose in my face.

"What?" I back away.

"You been drinking?"

"Dad!" I complain. "Where would I drink?"

"Just do it."

I breathe.

He wrinkles his nose. I'm worried he's going to take whatever bad breath I have for something more. Instead, he peers into my eyes. Finally he says, "You're late a lot."

I shrug, the movement sending shooting pains through my shoulder. I think I may have yanked it coming off the roof.

"Who were you hanging out with tonight?" Dad asks.

"No one." If this were a movie, the camera would do an extreme close-up on my face to show my guilt. I'm counting on Dad to not be that observant.

Still, he eyeballs me. His receding hair makes his wrinkling forehead more intense. Dad is able to give me "the look" right to the top of his scalp. It's unsettling. He puts his hands in the pockets of his cargo pants and pulls out a pamphlet. "Mr. Jefferson gave this to me today. He thought it might explain a few things about your behaviour." The pamphlet is titled *TIME TO ACT! Teen Drug and Alcohol Intervention*.

Thank you, Mr. Jefferson. So helpful. Now Dad thinks I'm a junkie.

I decide to ignore this latest assault on my credibility and get to my room before a real interrogation starts. "Listen, Dad," I say, "I have a test tomorrow morning, so . . ."

Actually it's the same social studies test I took today. The teacher said I can take it again if I study this time. What she doesn't understand is, I studied last time, for hours, and it didn't help. Still, I need to get my mark up or Dad will be asking for urine samples next. Besides, maybe one day I'll actually get a high enough grade to stop people from calling me stupid. It's worth a try.

There's a cheer from the TV, and Dad peeks back into the living room to see who scored. I start quickly down the hall, trying to get past

Dad before he wants to chat more. Bad move. He turns back and spots the camera.

"So, you have a test and instead of coming straight home to study, you decided to wander around with that stupid camera of yours."

His words wind around my heart and squeeze. Like a snake crushing my chest. "It's not stupid," I mutter.

"What the hell were you filming? More crappy Lego movies?" He has a chortle running under his words, mocking.

When I was a kid, a little kid, like maybe eight or so, I got into stop-motion animation for a while. I used the technique to make a bunch of *Star Wars* Lego films. I mean, everyone was doing it, and I was pretty proud of them. Dad didn't get it. He couldn't grasp the amount of time it took to shoot a two-minute sequence, even a crappy looking two-minute sequence. So, while my little sister Carly was winning lacrosse trophies and student-of-the-year awards, as far as Dad was concerned, I was wasting my time. It was a rocky start to my moviemaking career and one he hasn't quite gotten over.

"No, Dad. Not Lego."

"So — what, then?"

I think of the brick lit up by moonlight, the old tire looking like an eyeball, the lace-shadow from the fence, and I don't know how to explain it to him. Not in a way he would understand. Finally I say, "I was trying to show how different things appear in the moonlight."

"Moonlight, huh?" Dad looks at me like I'm crazy. He shakes his head dismissively. "Well, if you flunk out of school you can get a job with your mom at the flower shop. Flowers are like moonlight, right?"

I don't reply. Replying gives him ammo.

Annoyed by my silence, Dad continues, "You know if you spent half as much effort on school work as you do making your artsy-fart-sy films about moonlight and crap, you'd be on the honour roll like your sister. Or Pierce."

Screw Pierce. "Can I go now?" I sigh.

"Lose the attitude, Martin, or you're going

to lose a lot more," Dad threatens. He looks deep into my eyes again. "Are you sure you weren't . . .?"

"Just filming," I say.

"Fine." He turns back to the TV as another cheer rolls up.

I get to my room and close the door with a satisfying click. Pull my camera out of its bag. Slide into my office chair, spinning it toward my desk, take the memory card out of my camera, and plug it into my laptop all in a single practised motion. Then I download the results. Start looking through the clips, trying to find ways I can improve.

Most of the shots are awesome, but the focus is a little off on the bottle shot, and the light is a bit too intense in parts. It looked good in real life, but on the screen I'm losing details. Some of the jewel-like colours that were rebounding aren't as prominent. And it's not as three-dimensional as I want it to appear. I see how a simple change of angle could have dimmed the light and caught some of those colours and contours. I probably should have used a different lens, too.

I pull out my notebook and write the date and the subject. Then I start to make notes on what I've observed, so I won't make the same mistake again. I'm halfway through scribbling in my own personal shorthand when my doorknob turns. I flip my book over. I hate people looking at my writing. Especially my dad.

Carly bounces in. She's thirteen, going on fourteen, and deliberately annoying.

"What ya doin'?" she asks, smiling with silvery braces.

"Homework," I say.

She snatches up my notebook, looking it over and frowning. "What the heck kind of homework is this? Code class?"

"It's nothing. Just notes," I frown.

"For who? Aliens? Kindergarteners?" Her eyes sparkle with amusement.

"Nobody. Just me." I make a grab for my notebook, but Carly dances away flipping the pages.

"Ha, ha, this is crazy. You can even read this?"

"Give it back!" I make another grab, but she jumps on my bed.

"Are you sure you wrote this, because it looks like some preschooler just met the alphabet."

She turns the page roughly. I lunge. She dodges. There's a ripping sound, and the page flutters to the floor. Carly stops moving.

"Whoops, sorry."

My fingers wrap around her arm, and I raise my fist to her face. "You're dead." I growl.

"Do it and I'll scream," she warns, opening her mouth wide and looking right at me. Daring me.

I dart my fist at her head. She lets out a small squeal to show she's serious. I let go. I don't need Dad coming in here. Not with my footage still on the screen, and his princess ready to cry on demand. There's no way he'd side with me — even though Carly deserves every punch I've ever threatened her with.

"What do you want?" I ask, pulling the notebook out of her hand and picking the paper off the floor.

"I came to see if you wanted help with your school work. Need an essay written or something?"

"No essays right now, but I do have this social studies test to study for. Want to help with that?"

"Sure. That will be sixty bucks." My sister says, flipping her sandy hair over her shoulder, ice-blue eyes sparkling.

"Sixty bucks? That's a bit steep. You need that much makeup?"

Carly smacks my arm. "I want to get this cute dress I saw for the spring dance. I think Jamie will really like it. It's hot without being *hot* hot, you know?"

I sigh. "Saying a word twice doesn't change the meaning. It only makes you sound dumb."

"I'm the one who gets honours, just remember that."

I roll my eyes. "Whatever."

"So, do we have a deal?" She grins.

"I don't have sixty bucks."

"Too bad." Carly skips back to the door.

"You could help me anyway, out of the kindness of your heart."

Carly lets out a snort. "Sorry, bro."

"I could owe you."

"Naw. Cash upfront only. I'll try my puppy dog eyes on Daddy, instead. Mom is working late, and the Flames are ahead, so he'll probably give in."

"Why'd you ask to help me, then?"

"Helping you takes less effort than working Dad over. See ya!" Carly skips into the hall, then ducks her head back in. "If it works, I'll come back and give you a hand. It's quieter when you pass." Then she closes the door behind her.

I slot the page Carly ripped back into my notebook. She's right. My writing does look like that fake kid's stuff they put on ads to make it look cute. The kind with half the letters backward — except on those, the writing is neater.

I save all my footage to my computer and delete the files from my memory card, leaving it clean. Then I put the battery into the charger and load my spare charged battery into the camera, along with the freshly wiped memory card. Carefully I pack the camera away and put it on my bedside table.

Everything ready for my next shoot, I put my iTunes tracks on shuffle and crack open my social studies textbook. Under chapter eleven is the question: "To what extent does globalization contribute to sustainable prosperity for all people?" *Huh?* I don't even know what half those words mean. Actually, that's not quite right. I get each one of them on their own, but all together, it's like word soup. Not to mention the words pop out at me in the wrong order. It takes intense concentration to get them to all stay still long enough to read them as a sentence and by then my attention is too focused on doing that, instead of understanding what prosperity sustainable is, or whatever. I try to read the paragraph underneath, hoping it will all make sense by the time I'm done. Hoping to have it match up with what the teacher was talking about in class, which was actually pretty interesting. Fifteen minutes later, I'm done page one. I feel slightly motion sick, I'm totally exhausted, and I still don't understand what the paragraph is about.

It's probably because while I'm reading the words I keep thinking of something totally different. I imagine where I can shoot next, I remember what I had for supper, I think about that cute girl who came to our school for two days, then left again. I even end up singing along to a song that's playing. But, I can't focus. It's like my brain absorbs all the wrong things.

It's been this way my whole life. Words don't cooperate. I've always been able to cover it up, though. I mean, it's embarrassing to have so much trouble with something everyone else finds simple. I didn't want to be found out. In the early grades I learned the end of chapter questions were always in the order of the pages.

To answer the questions in my textbooks, all I had to do was match and copy. No major reading required. As I got older I would try to get kicked into the hall, so I could concentrate or at least be alone. In junior high I had to work even harder to hide my issues. I started "borrowing" answers from other kids until I was finally caught by a guy ten times bigger than me and threatened with a major beating. After that I fell into being the class clown, the easily excusable funny student. But, as the work got harder, nothing was really funny anymore. Then, this September rolled around and high school started. Without Carly helping me, I wouldn't be passing at all. No way in hell.

I decide to take a break from Social Studies and pull up Facebook. Stick's friend request is the first thing I see. I accept, then click on the message he's sent. I pray that he's not a big-time talker. I never read anything longer than a few sentences.

Turns out he's put a time (4:00 p.m.), a date (tomorrow), and an address with a link to Google Maps (Century Gardens). He's also put another link to a film contest with a note, "We could make a parkour movie."

I click the link. It goes to the Calgary Film Festival Youth by Youth contest. I give the site a quick look, my eyes darting corner to corner, picking up information at random. I click on the rules and entry form. It's long, but not too bad, until I hit the page with all the things I need to agree to. It's like my social studies textbook all over again. I catch words like copyright and ownership, but together, as a sentence, it doesn't really make sense. Exhaustion creeping in, I give up, clicking the red X in the corner of my screen. It doesn't matter, anyway. I don't need a contest or some board of judges telling me if my work is good enough. The likes on my YouTube channel do that.

I send a message back to Stick, *"See you tomorrow."*

I don't mention the contest.

4

STICK'S CREW

The C-train stops a block from Century Gardens, better known as Eighth and Eighth in downtown. To get into the park itself, I have to walk up the street, cross the road, and go onto the opposite C-train platform. From there I follow a wooden path. The first thing I see as I enter is a homeless guy drinking beer on a bench. He says something completely garbled, while pointing in my direction and winking. I clutch my camera to my chest and quicken my pace. On my left, four skateboarders are jumping and grinding by a fancy restaurant. Across a small pond, not yet filled with water, a girl has an enormous blue silk scarf strung in a tree. She climbs it and hangs upside-down, doing contortions above a worn gym mat. Nearby some ninjas train. I take out my camera and zoom in on them from the safety of my side of the pond. They flip and kick. Some of them even swing staffs. They're really cool. Stopping the video I continue walking, looking for Stick.

I finally see a couple of kids leaping around at the top of a huge concrete structure, which doubles as a crazily shaped water fountain in the summer. It's supposed to represent the Rocky Mountains coming down to Calgary. To me it looks more like giant concrete blocks smashed together. Still, it's kind of cool. There are a bunch of wooden walkways and stepping stones to get pedestrians through the art and from place to place.

Stick calls and waves from a bridge fifteen feet above me, then disappears. I follow the walkway under the bridge, coming to stand on the other side by a huge rock sticking through the two-by-fours. Stick is walking along the railing of the bridge like it's nothing. I get dizzy just looking. When he gets to the end, he hops down to a concrete wall five feet below, leaps over a gap, and across the path. He continues in a leaping, jogging loop around me from one handrail to the next. At one point he disappears behind a ledge before bounding back into view, flying a good seven feet, and stopping perfectly on a structure only six inches wide. After the roundabout journey he finally lands beside me, grinning. "You came!"

Now that I can get a good look at him in daylight and without adrenaline smashing through my veins, I can see how tall and wiry Stick is. He looks like he might be native or part native, and he's chiselled. Like every ounce of his body mass is used for muscle. I look down at my flabby gut and spongy arms and feel completely out of place, especially as more of his friends drop, literally drop, down around us.

"Hey, everyone, this is Martin. He's going to make a movie about us," Stick announces, wrapping his arm around my shoulder and jostling me.

"Um . . ." I start to explain how I'm not going to enter the contest, but Stick is already moving me into position.

"Look. James, Jovy, Sarah — you guys jump from here to here, right past the camera. Any style you want. We'll open the movie with that, okay? Then, Martin, you can film Vlad and me. We'll be coming from over there," Stick points up and follows the line all the way to the other side of the walkway. "Okay? Let's go."

The guys nod and run off. He looks at me. "Martin, ready?"

I shake my head. Anger shooting through my chest, constricting it. Stick didn't ask. He assumed. I feel used. "I'm not making the movie."

Stick's grin fades. "But, why?"

"I don't do contests." My face heats up. It's

probably nothing for Stick to read an entry form. But, for us stupid people . . .

Sweat beads under my fingertips, making the camera slippery in my grip. I want to leave. I'm awkward. Out of place.

"Okay," Stick says, his voice easy. "But, you like making films, don't you?"

"Well, yeah," I reply, "of course."

"Why?" He tilts his head. Waits for my answer.

That kind of stumps me. I mean, no one has ever asked me that before. I try to put all the thoughts I have about moviemaking into words. Make it so Stick can understand. "I like how things look through the camera," I explain. "I mean, you see a guy flying over you, right? Well, I can take that guy and make it so you not only see him, but you feel an emotion from it, too."

"You can do that?" Jovy asks, jumping down beside us again. "How?"

"It's all about using the right shots, angles, shadows, framing, direction, and a bunch of other stuff. A good director can take an ordinary shot, then using just visuals, can turn it into something ominous or sad or —"

"Epic!" James yells from above us.

"Yeah, exactly!" I grin.

"Can you do that for us?" Vlad asks.

"Yeah," Sarah says, squatting beside James above us, her long, brown hair blowing in the warm wind. "We could make our own YouTube channel."

"Will you?" Stick asks.

I finger my camera, little shards of excitement shooting through me, wiping away the discomfort. No one has ever been interested in my moviemaking before and no one's ever wanted me to do it for them.

I nod. "Absolutely. I'll make you guys look amazing."

"Great!" Stick says, "Let's get set up."

I take my camera out as Stick and his friends scramble away. Looking over the area, I choose my spot carefully, check the settings, then crouch and point the camera skyward, adjust the focus, and hit record. "Ready? Let's do this."

Jovy, Sarah, and James run one after the other in a J-shape. They each plant a foot on the side of a four-foot wall and leap off it in turn, flying through the air, arms stretching out to catch the concrete wall on the other side of the walkway with their fingers, like a cat or a monkey. Then they spin 180 degrees in mid-air, land on the ground, and run off in the direction they came from, their bright shirts a blur of colour.

Then it's Stick and Vlad's turn. I switch over to my telephoto lens and pan across as they follow another course, tracking around me. I spin and zoom to catch their leaps and mid-air somersaults across the gaps. They perform twists, grabs, and hurdles, often coming down on spaces I think are too small to land on. It's pretty incredible stuff. When it's over I adjust my position and tell everyone to do it again. In the course of the next hour I focus on faces, hands, feet. I shoot wide shots of bodies ping-ponging over obstacles. Then, with Stick's help get up higher, finding the best angle.

"Let me see what you did!" Jovy begs when we take a break.

I hold up the camera, so everyone can see, and press play.

"That is way sweet!" James calls out. "How do you do that?"

Sarah nods. "We shot a video and it was crap compared to this stuff."

I tell them about how I chose the shot. Picked the lighting. I talk about framing. I describe the effects I can add afterward and the music I can get. I tell them about their future YouTube channel and how they'll be able to see themselves there in a few days, once the editing is done. The group is pretty excited about that. And I have to keep wondering if I'm having a dream. I can't believe people are interested in what I have to say. That *I'm* teaching *them*. It's cool.

"Shoot this!" James says. "Come on." He climbs up the structure to the top and disappears over an angled chunk of concrete. I look for a way to follow him.

"Go that way." Stick points behind him. "Still don't want to enter the movie contest?"

"No."

"What if I find a different one? Something more basic? No high stakes?" Stick follows me up, balancing on the banister. "I mean, I get that you only film for fun. But, a contest might be fun too. You know?"

I wrack my head to find a way to get out of it, but Stick looks so hopeful. I see it means a lot to him. *Maybe I could enter something. Just this once.* "Okay," I say. "But, only if you can find a contest with almost no entry form."

Stick nods. "I totally get you, man. I hate paperwork more than you know."

I go to film James, leaving Stick behind, typing on his phone. Fifteen minutes later, he brings it over to me. "How about this one?"

I look at it. It's a local video contest put out by Youth Central called All About Me In Calgary.

I scan the entry form. It consists of a name, age, and e-mail address. Nothing more. But, the contest is supposed to be about myself. My view of the world as a teen growing up in Calgary. I don't know if it would work as a parkour movie. And as for filming my life — *what is there to know?* My dad tells me I'm stupid. My teachers hate me. Every word I read twists and moves. Leaps and turns. Nothing in my head stands still. Not right or left or up or down. It won't work. It can't . . .

I look over and watch James flipping from one stepping stone to the next. He looks like the inside of my head. In fact, all of Stick's friends jumping around, twisting in mid-air, leaping from point to point without setting down anywhere, it *all* matches the jumble that is my brain.

Actually, parkour might work.

"Okay," I say to Stick. "I'll do it. But, it's not going to be *just* about parkour. It's going to be bigger than that. And it's going to win."

"Awesome!" Stick beams.

We bump fists, and the deal is done.

5

SNAPPED

I'm feeling pretty pumped by the time I hit my house. There's an electric buzz flowing through my veins. Stick's crew thought I was smart. Not just smart, a genius. That's what Sarah called me, anyway. My moviemaking was important to these guys. Until I came, their usual method of gathering footage was to plonk down a cheap point-and-shoot camera somewhere and let it roll. They had never seen the kinds of stuff I was able to pull off.

I even managed to impress myself.

I glance at my watch. Five minutes early. No reason for Dad to freak out or accuse me of whatever he was getting at last night. And I'm going to get right to work on the novel we're supposed finish for English tomorrow, so he can't say I'm slacking, either. Of course I'm not *actually* going to read the novel. I'll just see if they have the movie on Netflix or YouTube. After that, I'll work on my math assignment. It's only twenty questions long. That should take me about an hour. I might even be able to slip in some editing time if I get done quickly enough. I also have to figure out how I'm going to put this movie entry together. Match the parkour moves to the things I experience in my life. That's going to be the tough part.

I dig into my backpack and pull out my redone social studies test. Sixty-four per cent. Awesome. Of course, Carly did help me study. And the teacher explained a question I was hanging over for five minutes. I think she got tired of watching me sit there. Still, I nailed most of the multiple choice questions on my own. The two long-answer parts gave me a bit of trouble, but I remembered what the teacher was talking about in class and basically copied what she said. In the end, I got my best mark ever.

I head toward my room, happy.

A cup flies past my ear and bounces off the wall behind me, spattering the floor with rancid milk and chips of earthenware.

"Hey!" I yell, startled. "Carly?"

But, it's not my sister. Dad is ripping my room to bits. My mattress has been turned on its side against the wall. Blankets snake over the floor. Most of my dresser drawers are open with clothes hanging out. My books, all six of them, have been flung and lie on my box spring. All my DVD cases are open, and the disks are everywhere. Even my notebook, with its scrawls, hasn't been spared. My wastepaper basket has been dumped, and chip bags, gum wrappers, and old school work mix in with my blankets. Dad has his back to me. What hair he has is sticking up. He snatches my large camera bag with my lenses and extra equipment in it off the floor and begins to open it.

"Dad!"

He spins, bag dangling from his fist. Right then I'm thankful I have my actual camera on me, still in its travel bag; though, the contents of the bag that swings in Dad's hand are easily worth four thousand dollars. Easily. And he looks like he might hurl it at the wall.

"What are you doing?" I gasp.

"I'm tired of this garbage!" Dad yells. "Bad grades, coming in late, not talking more than two words to me or your mother. So, where are they?"

"What are you talking about?"

"Drugs."

The word slams me like a train out of nowhere. "What the fuck?"

"Watch your language!" Dad snaps.

He's accusing me of using drugs, and I should watch my language? My head swims. I'm off kilter. Like I've had too many corn dogs at the Calgary Stampede, then ridden The Slingshot.

"Where are they?" Dad screams again, obviously at the end of his tether. I wonder how long he's been searching.

I rub my hand over my face.

Dad swings the camera bag, waiting.

Chants of, *Please don't break, please don't break*, repeat silently beneath my lips.

"Well? Are you going to tell me?" Dad growls.

"Ritalin is the only drug I take," I reply. "Not that I need it," I add in a low mutter.

Even though I'm trying to calm my dad down, get him to give me my bag, I find a bitterness creeping into my voice. Anger.

"Ritalin helps you," Dad says.

"Then, why am I still failing?"

Dad's face goes red, right to his receding hairline. "That's what I'm trying to find out!" He grabs my notebook up off the floor. "I mean, look at this writing! Is it supposed to be a joke? Only a complete stoner would write like this and —" He grabs some of the crumpled papers that have flown out of my garbage can. "Fifty-two in Math. Twenty per cent in English? Even an ESL kid could get better marks than this. If you tried — really tried —" Dad swings the lens bag again in frustration. The lenses clatter against each other.

"Dad, could you put the bag down?"

Dad looks at his hand. I think he forgot the bag was there. "Why? So you can waste time playing with toys, instead of studying?" Dad huffs. "Ritalin can only do so much. You have to make an effort, too. You have to take responsibility. This," he shakes the bag, "is a distraction." Dad looks at me, his eyes red along the bottom. "Martin, don't you understand? Your mom and I want you to —"

"Be something I'm not." I finish for him, trying to make him understand. Trying to find the right words. "But I'm not like you, or Mom, or Pierce, I'm —"

I was going to say *a filmmaker*, but Dad ends my sentence with something else. The same thing he always ends with.

"Stupid."

The word goes off like a firecracker in my head. Impulsively I snatch at the camera bag, grabbing onto the strap and yanking, my white knuckles next to his. "Don't say that!"

"Then, buckle down!" Dad says. "When you fail, it's like I've . . . It's embarrassing."

"I don't care!" I yell, my own frustration cracking my voice.

"Well, you should!" Dad pulls back on the bag, his face twisting with annoyance and anger. The lenses shudder fearfully, like bones knocking into one another. The snap of glass brings us both to a halt.

Something inside me breaks with that sound. "Get the hell out of my room!" I scream.

Dad drops the strap and walks away, back wet with sweat. I slam the door behind him, closing my eyes and waiting for the squeezing around my heart to ease off.

Finally, when my fingers have stopped trembling enough that I can trust myself with my own equipment, I put the bag on the box spring of my bed and unzip the top. Gently I take the lenses out and lay them on my comforter, one by one, examining the equipment. My wide-angle lens is fine. My regular focus and my macro are both good too, as are the other four lenses I look at. Then, I start pulling out all the other stuff. Hoping for the best. Finally I find what made the cracking noise. My blue lens filter is broken. I exhale for the first time in five minutes. That's easy to replace. The filter is under ten bucks at any camera shop, probably less on eBay. Carefully I put everything back into my bag and hide it under a pile of clothes in the back of my closet. Then I download the parkour footage from today onto my computer, scrub the memory card, switch the battery, and hide the camera too. I decide to leave my room a mess. I'm kind of hoping Mom will come home and see it. She'll take my side. I'm sure of that. She hates it when Dad loses his temper.

Finally I get to my homework. Reading, or in my case viewing, *To Kill a Mockingbird* by Harper Lee. I know a bit about this movie. It was filmed in 1962 and starred Gregory Peck. That year the film won three Academy Awards. One of them was for the best art direction. So, I'm kind of interested in checking it out, anyway. Maybe I can improve some of my skills while also doing my homework. A win-win for everyone. But, I'm also intrigued by the story. The parts the teacher read in class were really good. I can't wait to see how it ends.

6

DRUG BUST

The bell rings for the start of classes. I have English 10-1 first thing. The highest level of English class you can take without being an International Baccalaureate student, better known as an IB. I am not an IB. I'm not even an English 10-1 no matter what Dad wants to believe. I drag my butt to class and find my desk. I'm lucky to have one. They had to track down a few more at the beginning of the semester. Too many kids, not enough teachers. At least that keeps the focus off of me, for the most part. Especially since Dad fought at the beginning of the year to get me put in all the upper-level classes, determined that I have what I need to go to university. I shouldn't be here.

I have no intention of going to university.

Mrs. Rogers, our teacher, starts by talking about the novel. The movie last night was really good, until Dad came storming in accusing me of slacking. When I tried to explain how what I was watching was homework, he slammed my laptop shut, dumped my backpack, and shoved the book into my hands. Then he stood over me, watching while I read and ranting that I wasn't turning the page fast enough. Finally he said he had enough of my dicking around and flipped off the light before I even got to my math homework. I had to put my bed back together in the dark. To top it all off, Mom was working really late again.

I burned all night long.

Now, I don't even know half of what Mrs. Rogers is talking about. Not that it matters. I'm probably going to fail this class, anyway. I tune out and start to storyboard my movie. I'm sketching a close-up of Stick's half-shadowed face, when Mrs. Rogers decides to make an example out of me. She tells me, since I can't pay attention, I have to stand up in front of the room and read the end of the novel to the class. At first I don't move. My pits sweat. My heart thuds. I cross my arms over my chest and shake my head. I'm hoping my fight will make it too much trouble for her to bother with me and she'll move on. Then she mentions the principal's office and calling my parents. A winning move.

I drag myself all the way to the front of the room.

Opening to the wrong page first because I reversed the numbers doesn't make Mrs. Rogers or the go-getters in the class any happier. I can see it in their faces. I'm just wasting their time. I clear my throat. Try to cut off the shuffling feet and snickers. Try to read the words dancing on the page.

For me, reading is like building a tower of blocks on a wobbly table. I start the sentence, working hard to keep it all in order, balancing everything. And if it's quiet and calm, sometimes things go well. Right now, I read slowly and everything comes out right. I start to think this isn't going to be so bad, when someone shouts, "You read like a robot!" and the whole thing collapses. My eyes dart. It takes me some time to find my place again. When I do, the first word I say is followed by the last one in the line.

Will home you take me?

Laughter erupts, and someone from the back of the class hoots. I try the sentence again. It doesn't get any better.

Will me you take home?

I squint. Try to concentrate harder. It makes no difference.

Will whispered you take me?

Somehow a word from the sentence below jumps up into the middle of the sentence I'm reading, making a mangled train wreck of meaning.

I finally get the sentence to lie down and

behave, and things go okay for a bit. Then I hit a word I've never seen before and I'm forced to sound it out, syllable by syllable. Slowly, painfully, like some Grade One brat.

Ah — zah — lee — as

People are laughing really hard now. I look up to see half the class rolling their eyes and the other half in tears. I know what they're thinking. I'm stupid or I'm doing this on purpose as a joke. I decide the latter is a better alternative. So, I go off script. Use the word I'm working on to launch into an annoying top forty song my sister croons out every chance she gets. By the second verse I have half the class singing along with me. By the third I'm back in my desk, working on my movie, the teacher having given up on me.

"If you practised reading as much as drawing, Martin," Mrs. Rogers says, "you might improve. And if you need help just come and see me."

A couple of kids snicker. My face burns. I'll never go see her. Never.

I sketch with trembling hands.

"Now, class, please copy this down." Mrs. Rogers writes on the white board with a squeaky marker. "Thanks to Martin and his disruption, we won't have time for a class discussion about the novel. So instead, I want you to write a minimum five-page overview, covering these things, due Monday."

The class groans. Mrs. Rogers is lying. I know she was going to assign the essay anyway.

I copy down the assignment, but I don't really get it. Something about controlling ideas, narrative detail, and conflict development. I'm hoping Carly will understand, but I'm not sure they teach those things in junior high. *I* don't remember taking it. Still, having Carly write the essay for me is the only way I'll be able to get a high enough mark to keep Dad off my back. And for that, I need money. Luckily, I have York. I shoot him a text from under the desk right as the bell rings.

The class slumps into the hall. Someone

pushes me into the row of lockers. "Nice song," he snorts. "See you in Gym." In the classroom beside ours the kids from English 10-2, the class I should have been in, are streaming out too. They get to act out the books they read. They make movies and do PowerPoint presentations. I've even heard that sometimes they sit in a circle and discuss what they thought of the books, instead of writing it out. If I were in that class, I might have a better mark, and even if I didn't, it sounds a lot more interesting than essay after stupid essay.

I go to my locker and put away my English books, exchanging them for gym clothes. I also grab my full bottle of Ritalin, giving the pills a shake before putting it in my pocket. Then, I head for the mural. York is waiting there, as planned.

"Hey, G!" York says, bro-fisting me as I arrive. "Got my vitamin R?"

York talks like a big, black guy from some made-for-TV movie. He is really a freckle-faced redhead from St. Catharines, Ontario, who moved here three years ago. I've been selling him my Ritalin nearly that long. He buys the pills from me at five dollars per twenty-gram pill, then resells the pills for eight dollars apiece. I've bought a lot of essays and camera equipment with these little pills, so I guess Dad was right, they have improved my life.

I hold out my bottle to York, who takes it, looking appreciative. "Nice load, boy. How much are you willing to part with?"

I never sell my whole bottle. I have to have some to show Dad. In case he makes me take my dose in front of him. Of course, when that happens, I slip the pill into my cheek and spit it in the toilet. I haven't taken my Ritalin for a long, long time.

I was first prescribed the stuff when my grade eight teacher insisted my parents put me on it to help me concentrate. The pill-happy doctor I was dragged to glossed over the attention-deficit/hyperactivity disorder (ADHD) questionnaire. I didn't even answer most of the questions. The doctor seemed happy to let my parents answer for me. Then, he wrote up the meds. A little pill to make all my problems go away. Just like magic.

I took the pills for four months.

Ritalin made me anxious. I couldn't eat. I couldn't sleep. My heart felt like it was always racing. Mom took me back to the doctor after I dropped twenty pounds in three weeks. He said it wasn't anything to worry about since I was overweight to begin with. Meanwhile the teacher, happy that I was now medicated, wrote a glowing report for the doctor based on nothing as far as I could tell and then left me alone. No extra help. No teacher's assistant. Just take the pill and get back to work. But nothing improved, so I quit taking them. That was right around the time York hit me up. He wasn't the only one. I'd already had two other offers to buy my prescription. York offered me the best price.

"I can sell you most of them," I say, leaning against the wall. "How about forty pills?"

York squints, making his nose paler and his dark freckles more noticeable. "Can you get away with that?"

"Sure," I reply. "No problem."

"Parents are so stupid."

"Tell me about it." I give York the short version of last night's mayhem, complete with the room destruction, the rebounding cup, and the violation of my camera equipment. "My dad doesn't even realize that he's my primary drug dealer. Him and the doctor."

"This guy." York taps the label on the bottle. "He's on a good half of the pills I sell. He must get kickbacks or something."

"Yeah, he seemed pretty eager to drug me up. So forty pills, that's —" I take out my phone and use the calculator. I can't hold numbers in my head. The calculations always end up in a square dance. "Two hundred dollars."

"Cool," York says, "I'll get it to you by Monday."

I snatch the bottle back. "No way! I need the money now."

"Come on!" York holds out his hands. "That's a lot of dough. I'm tapped out."

"Well, so am I."

"You know I'm good for the cash. What's the issue?"

I do trust York. I've been dealing with him for long enough that I know he won't screw me. But Carly only works on a cash-upfront basis. The essay is due on Monday. I need the money now.

"Don't you have anything?" I ask. "I'll give you all forty if you can advance me eighty dollars. I need something."

"Sorry, G. I have all my cash wrapped up in NOS and X for a big party this weekend. I won't see any profit until that's over. Come on, you know I can move your stuff quick."

I shake my head. "I can't." I wonder what my chances are if I sell the pills myself. There are always a few guys hunting around for vitamin R.

York seems to know what I'm thinking and opens his mouth to warn me off when Vice

Principal Dixon strides up and grabs us both by the shoulders. York narrows his eyes. His nostrils flare.

"Get your hands off of me!" York snaps, twisting away.

I don't move. Instead, I stand there, clutching my bottle of Ritalin and wishing it was still in my locker. I'm praying York freaks out enough that I can at least get the stuff into my pocket before Mr. Dixon sees it.

Luck is not on my side.

"What do we have here?" Mr. Dixon snatches the bottle out of my hand.

I try to explain, say something, get out of trouble, but my brain is a stew of unrelated words.

York just glares.

"Office," Mr. Dixon commands. Hand on each of our shoulders like he expects us to run, we're led to the main office and told to sit in the chairs outside the principal's lair.

Mr. Dixon knocks and lets himself in. We listen as he explains how he broke up our drug ring. How money was being flashed. How pills were being exchanged. He makes it sound really bad. The principal sticks his head out of the office and tells the secretary to call our parents. He wants them in immediately. He says he might even have to contact the police.

I know this is for our benefit. He could have called the secretary on his phone. It's a threat we were meant to hear. And it's working. York and I look at each other, blood draining from our faces.

7

THE PRINCIPAL'S OFFICE

York's dad arrives first, fingering the thick leather belt that cinches his pants around his wiry waist. A sourness wafts off him as he passes, entering the principal's office. York looks at his lap, his fingers white, twined into each other.

Both my mom and dad arrive together. Dad must have picked up mom from work — or vice versa. Mom's face is pinched. She says she's never been a fan of school or the principal's office. It's why Dad is always the one who deals with my scholastic issues. Things must be bad for Mom to be here. Especially during wedding and prom season. Not much can drag her away from the floral business during wedding and prom season. Dad is furious. His forehead wrinkles all the way up to the middle of his scalp. I'm doomed.

The door is pulled closed behind them.

"Well, fuck," York mutters. "Dad actually showed."

"Ditto," I say. "What do you think they're going to do to us?"

"The school? Who cares? My dad, he's going to beat the living hell out of me."

"We didn't even do anything," I grumble. "Not like Mr. Dickwad says, anyway."

"Like that matters."

"But . . . but . . ." I brighten. "We didn't *do* anything."

"Yeah, you said that," York growls.

"Think about it," I say.

"I am. I'm dead any way I look at it."

"Whose pills were they?" I ask.

"Yours."

"And who had them?"

York slumps. "You, but who cares? Mr. Dickwad can say I had them."

"But, all the pills are still in the bottle. Nothing was taken out. His story doesn't work," I reason.

"He could say he put them back in," York counters.

"Fine. But, where's the money?" I say. "He said we flashed it."

York goes from grim to grinning in milliseconds. "Where *is* the money? I'm still broke. You?"

"My pockets are empty."

York links his fingers behind his head and leans back, runners sticking out in front of him, crossed at the ankles. "Martin, you're a genius. We're golden."

It's the second time I've been called a genius in two days. I start laughing. I'm still laughing when we're ushered into the office. In fact, I have trouble stopping.

"Something funny?" the principal asks, frowning.

"No. No," I mutter, trying to keep a straight face.

York and I stand by the bookshelf of the small office, made smaller by the five adults all staring at us. My bottle of Ritalin sits on the desk.

York's dad clears his throat and adjusts himself in his chair. "Let's get on with this. I'm losing money every second I'm not on the job." He glares at York. "Are you a god-damned druggie?"

York shakes his head. "I don't touch the stuff."

I have to force myself to not start laughing again. York isn't lying. He sells drugs, lots of them, but he doesn't do them himself.

Mr. Dixon *ah-hems* and begins his speech. "Lately, there have been issues with Ritalin and other prescription drugs getting into the hands of our non-medicated students." He motions toward York. "And now I think we know who is at the heart of this problem."

"Prove it," York sneers.

"What happened?" my mom asks, looking

right into my eyes, hoping this is all a mistake.

I play my own truth card. "I was showing York my pills."

"Why?" the principal says.

"Well, my dad ripped my room apart looking for drugs, and I was wondering if York agreed that Ritalin *was* a drug. I mean it's the only drug I take, and my dad's the one who makes me take it." Cue the wide, innocent eyes. Close-up on the brimming tears.

My mom turns on my dad, exclaiming, "You ripped Martin's room apart? When?"

Bingo. Pan wide to see Dad sweat.

"Last night," he says, practically under his breath.

I pour on the drama. Bring home the scene. "He threw a cup against the wall, tipped my bed over, and went through my garbage. He nearly wrecked my camera equipment too. Some of those were Grandma's old lenses. The ones she put in her will." I know I'm pushing the poor-me card a bit close to the edge with that last bit, but I figure it's worth a try.

My dad's face goes bright red. "I was just . . . he's been . . . I was looking for . . ." he sputters.

"That's a terrible violation of his privacy," Mom scolds. "I can't believe you did that."

Dad throws up his hands. "If he's having trouble, it's my job to help him."

"Not like that," Mom says.

Dad looks at his lap, mad. "We'll talk about this when we get home."

"Damn right we will." Mom folds her hands in her lap, lips tight, chin high.

"The point is, Mr. Dixon scowls, "the boys were buying and selling drugs in school, and we —"

"No, we weren't," York says, coolly bringing the focus back on us.

"I saw you." Mr. Dixon says.

"You saw me with the pills. But, where's this money you said we had?" I ask.

"Yes," the principal says. "Do you have that, Mr. Dixon?"

Mr. Dixon falters before finally spitting out, "I didn't get my hands on that yet."

"Empty your pockets!" York's dad yells out. "Empty your pockets, and let's be done with it. I don't have all day to jaw."

York empties his pockets first. He has a couple of granola bar wrappers, an opened pack of balloons, a condom, and two safety pins.

"Now, you, boy!" York's dad points his gnarled finger at me. It shakes.

I pull out a folded piece of paper with movie shots on it, a pen, and some pocket lint. Nothing else.

"I know what I saw," Mr. Dixon grumbles.

York narrows his eyes. "Are you sure?"

York's dad gets up and grabs his jacket off the back of his chair. "I have work to do. Real work. Not this chasing leprechauns stuff." He goes out the door, closing it so hard the frosted glass rattles.

"You may have misread the situation," the principal says to Mr. Dixon.

"I don't think I did," Mr. Dixon replies, his eyes not leaving York.

The principal clears his throat. "Well for

now, boys, get a pass from the secretary and return to your classes. Martin, in the future, please keep your medication to yourself, so we don't have these kinds of issues." He hands me back my bottle.

I nod.

York and I gather up our things and leave. I hear my parents start talking as the door closes. I'd love to stay and listen, but I have other things to do. Out in the hall and around the corner, I pop open the bottle. "How about five pills for one essay," I say. "Can you do that?"

"Is that all you want?" York asks. "No problem. I have some IB's who owe me money. I'll get one of them to work it off, instead."

"So, we have a deal?"

"We have a deal. Send me the topic, and I'll have it to you by . . ."

"Sunday," I answer.

"Sunday. No problem. Nice doing business with you," he says.

8

RUNNING

It's Friday by the time I see Stick and his crew again. I haven't got much editing done. Now that Dad is finally convinced I don't use drugs, he thinks I must have oppositional defiance disorder, coupled with a complete lack of self-discipline. Thanks to Google search, and its wonderful parenting advice, I've spent the last few days doing my homework in the living room under Dad's eagle eye with the hockey game blaring in the background.

I see how disappointed everyone is about their first parkour video not being up and I promise to get it done by Sunday. That should be easy enough with York taking care of the essay. Still, to take the heat off me, I decide to entertain everyone with the story of my trip to the principal's office. I figure it will be good for a few laughs if nothing else. But as I start describing it, Stick crosses his arms.

". . . so, then Mr. Dickwad, our vice principal who's had it out for York since he hit the school, is backpedalling and telling the principal how he's not wrong. And there are both our parents, glaring at him like they want to do him in. Really throttle him. Especially York's dad."

"Yeah?" Stick says, interrupting. "Great. So, are we shooting or what?"

Tough crowd. Honestly, I thought he'd get a kick out of the story.

"Well," I say looking around. "How about I shoot from underneath the stepping stones? You guys can all jump over me, and I'll lie on my back."

"What part of the script is this?" Stick asks.

The world zooms in on me. A close-up on

my agitation. "I don't write scripts," I frown. "I work with a storyboard."

"Can I see?"

I show Stick the sketches I've been making. I've ticked off the ones that we've finished shooting. We're about halfway done.

"You misspelt that word," Stick says, pointing at the few notes that line the margins. "And that d is backward. So is that one."

"So, what?" I fold up the paper and shove it into my back pocket.

Stick runs up the wall beside us and back flips to his feet. "But, in the e-mail you said you were going to do a voice-over, too. When will that be written?"

"I was going to wing it," I reply.

Stick heaves a breath, "Whatever."

He heads off to the stepping stones, and I follow, the only one using the stairs. Once there I climb down into the deep pit, a place normally filled with water once the weather gets warm. There are little puddles where the freak spring snowstorm of two days ago has melted. I lie down in one of the dryer patches and adjust my focus to maximize the back-lighting. I want the crew to look like shadows, not people.

"Okay, go," I call.

Over and over again they fly. I zoom, then shoot wide. I blur the focus. It looks pretty cool.

"Can we see?" James asks as I climb out.

I replay the shots. Stick hangs back.

"Are you going to be able to get our stuff up and still make the contest deadline?" Sarah asks.

"Oh yeah," I say. "My sister, Carly, said she would keep Dad busy this weekend, so I can have a break. She's already told me her plan is to bug him until he can't take it anymore. So basically that will mean no parental super-vision for a whole two days, at least."

"You should be grateful," Stick says.

"About what?" I demand.

"At least you have a dad who . . ."

". . . gets in my face every two seconds?

Why should I be grateful about that?"

Stick waves his hand, turning away. "Never mind. Let's just get this done."

"Fine." I pull out my storyboard and look at it, glancing over my shoulder to make sure Stick isn't checking my spelling again. He's not. He's climbed up to the bridge and is precision jumping between the two rails. It looks completely dangerous. "Hey, Stick," I call to him. "Can you somersault in mid-air and hold on to something?"

He shrugs. "I think so. Let me try." He hops down, grabs his water bottle, and flips on the spot. "No problem."

"How about with the camera?"

"How heavy is it?"

I hand it to him, fingertips tingling as I give it away.

He hefts it up and down in one hand. "Yeah, I can do it. I'll put the strap around my neck too, just in case."

"Alright, let's try shooting from your perspective."

Stick grins. The first one I've seen since I've arrived. "Awesome."

I take the camera back and set up the focus, then get it rolling. I hand it to him and watch him put the strap over his neck while my heart thumps in my throat. "Don't drop it. Okay?"

"Don't worry."

"Or bump it into anything."

"I'll be careful." Stick climbs one-handed onto a ledge.

I hold my breath.

"Ready?" he calls.

"The camera is rolling. Go ahead."

He leans forward and runs, skipping across the tops of ledges and over gaps until he's a good thirty feet away. With every step I see a trip. That's what would happen if it were me doing this. I'm the clumsiest, most uncoordinated person on the planet. But, Stick, it's like he's magnetized to the concrete. His fingers press hard against the camera's black body. He leaps over gap after gap. Then, he turns. Runs back toward us, plants his feet on a ledge, his body flipping — feet over head. I dread that he won't land it. I dread that he'll slip, and I'll hear the tinkle of a million tiny pieces of plastic and metal scattering over a splatter of blood.

But, he lands it two-footed on the ground and jumps into two more amazing flips, then keeps running, doing trick after trick — a one-handed vault, a dive into a shoulder roll, hitting the wall with one hand and spinning his body around it. Finally he circles back and drops down beside me from the ledge above. "Here you go."

"Thanks," I say, taking the camera and trying to pull air back into my lungs while checking it over for any damage. It's fine. Perfectly fine.

We all look at the footage. It's insane. The craziest thing I've ever seen. It looks like the world is whirling in a clothes drier.

"Hey, Stick —" I'm about to say more, but my phone rings. I pull it out of my pocket and have a look at it. It's Dad. "Sorry, I have to get this."

Stick shrugs and jogs off to run a loop.

"Hi, Dad," I answer.

"Where are you?" he demands, his voice tight.

"Um, at the park."

"What park?"

"Century Gardens, you know Eighth and Eighth, downtown."

"Why the heck are you there?"

"Filming," I say, hoping to lessen some of his fears. I know what Dad is thinking. This area is known for its drug trade.

"Sure," Dad grunts.

"What do you want?" I sigh.

"I need you home. Now."

"Why?" I look at my watch. I'm not late, yet. Close, if I don't leave soon, but not yet.

"My boss, Mr. Jefferson, invited us over for a barbeque."

"What?"

"It's a big opportunity," Dad huffs. "Besides, you'll finally get to meet Pierce. It's not like you're doing anything important, anyway."

My jaw clamps shut.

Dad continues, "Half an hour — be here or be grounded, got it?"

"Fine." I hang up.

"Who was that?" Stick asks, leaping down beside me and making me jump.

"My dad," I say. "He's such an asshole. I wish he'd just screw off."

Stick doesn't say anything. He looks like he's frozen. Then, his face collapses in an angry scowl and he whispers, "You don't even know what you have." He turns and runs. Not over the concrete or in some fancy parkour way. A straight sprint, out to the sidewalk and away.

"Wait!" I call.

His crew leaps over to me.

"What happened?" Vlad asks.

"I don't know," I say. Because I honestly don't. I must have crossed a line, but, really, I'm not sure what it was.

9

GUILT

It's Sunday night. Two days since our *lovely* supper with the Jeffersons. At least Dad saw Pierce for who he was — a kiss-up with no personality. He couldn't stop telling Mom all the way home how his potted plant at the office was more interesting than Pierce. I guess the love fest is over. Maybe now I'll catch a break, and Dad will go back to leaving me alone.

I heave a sigh as I go through the 161 individual video clips. I end up watching the one with the spinning paper over and over again. It's a crumpled piece of notebook I found blowing around the schoolyard, stuck in a mini tornado with dust and candy wrappers. There are bright blue and pink highlighter marks on it, and I can make out the word *AWESOME* written in all capital letters. The word blurs and twists in the wind.

Finally I go on to the next clip, but not before making a note on what to do with the paper. The next shot is of Stick flipping. I splice in a shattering effect right before he lands, then transition to the shot of the black tire, letting the dark take over the screen. I play that section through again. The crack in the sidewalk. A weed pushing through. James doing a handstand on a ledge, looking like he's come out of nowhere. Stick's footage of him, spinning through the air. Everyone flying backlit against the blue sky. The tornado of garbage with *AWESOME* twisting around. Stick running past, flipping, shattering, the tire, blackness.

It's looking great. I know I have at least six to eight more hours of editing to do before

I'm even close to putting in the sound, but the whole movie is making me high with anticipation. I can't see how I can lose this All About Me In Calgary contest. This is going to blow the judges away. Unfortunately, Stick is right about one thing. I'm going to have to write a script. A voice-over part to pull it all together. Winging it probably won't work.

I've never thought about putting my life into words before. Pictures are always an easier way for me to communicate. But, that doesn't work for most people. It seems like the majority of the population wants things explained in plain, clear vocabulary. And that makes me anxious.

I look back at my plans for the shoot. There's only one more scene to finish the movie. But, for that I need Stick and I haven't seen or heard from him since he stormed off on Friday.

It's weird, I've only known him for a week, but we've talked nearly every night since that first shoot at Century Gardens, discussing movies, parkour tricks, and how we could shoot the most epic scenes. He gets me. Unfortunately, I think I don't get him. Not in the way he wants. I've done something, said something, which has completely thrown him off his game. Only I don't know what it was.

And I don't know how to repair it.

Since the incident he hasn't answered any of my messages on Facebook, my texts, or my voice mail. He wasn't even at the parkour jam this afternoon that James says he never misses. I went down there looking for him, feeling all stalkerish. I'm twisted up with guilt. And not just because of my movie. The thing is, as pathetic as it sounds, Stick is the only real friend I've had in a long while — and it took me a whole week to screw it up.

At least he hasn't blocked me. I check Facebook again to see if Stick is on. He's not. I leave it up, running in the background while I piece together the last of the parkour video I made of the extra footage I'm not going to be using for my film. The shots are crazy, and I manage to get the movement to flow, so it looks like tides in the ocean. Or at least that's the way it looks to me. I add some funky dubstep music and upload the whole thing onto the crew's brand-new YouTube channel.

Loading takes forever.

There's a ping from Facebook before the loading bar is even at twelve per cent. My heart speeds up. I really hope it's Stick.

It's not. York has sent my English essay as an attachment. I download it from the Web and open it up. The thing is dense. It's full of big words and complex arguments. It goes over the entire *To Kill a Mockingbird* novel. I try my best to read it. But, as bad as I am on paper, I'm ten times worse reading off the screen. After spending a good twenty minutes — eyes leapfrogging from one word to the next, and usually not in order — I finally give it a pass. It sounds like the same BS the teacher spouts. It should get me at least a sixty or seventy per cent. Enough to pull up my average and keep Dad off Google search for a while. I don't need him diagnosing me with anything else.

I put my name on the essay and send it to the printer, then check the upload on the parkour video. It's just finishing up when there's another ping. I figure it's York, making sure I got the essay, but this time it's Stick. I quickly read over what he's written — an address with the words, "7:30 tomorrow."

I go to reply, but he's already off line. I'm wondering what I'm going to be faced with when I see him. It's kind of freaking me out.

But, I'm still going.

10

STICK'S PAST

The address isn't a park like I was thinking. It's not even by a park. It's a house. A decent-sized one, too. From the outside it looks well-kept. A big front door with mottled glass panes, dark brown stucco, and a couple of impressive flower gardens hedged in by shrubs. I ring the doorbell, then realize I don't remember Stick's real name. I did see it on his Facebook page, but now it's kind of gone from my memory.

Panic really sets in when I see a woman's shape coming to answer the door. I wrack my brain. Nothing. I think it might start with an

A — maybe. I really hope his parents call him Stick too or this is going to be totally embarrassing.

The woman opens the door and greets me with a tentative smile, like she's not really sure if I'm friend or foe. It's kind of a strange reaction. She has long, brown hair and large brown eyes. She's thin and probably in her mid-thirties. Maybe. And she doesn't look anything like Stick. "Can I help you?" she asks.

"Uh," I'm not sure what to say. Suddenly I'm worried I'm at the wrong address. That I've written the numbers down in the wrong order. It isn't like that hasn't happened before. And I'm still not sure if I should ask for Stick or make an attempt at hopefully blurting out his real name just in case I am at the right place.

"Hey, Martin!" Stick appears over the woman's shoulder. "It's okay, Gloria. He's a friend of mine. I invited him over. We're working on a project. I hope that's okay."

The woman, Gloria, finally gives me a real smile, a big one. "Oh that's fine, Alan. Come on in, Martin. Nice to meet you."

She puts out her hand, and we shake. Her grip is soft, but secure. Somehow it doesn't surprise me that Stick calls his mom by her name. He seems like that kind of guy. I take off my shoes and relinquish my coat to Gloria, who hangs it in a well-organized closet. The foyer leads into a big living room. There are two couches, two arm chairs, a coffee table with a vase of flowers on it and a widescreen TV. Three boys, all between nine and twelve years old, are playing Wii archery in front of it. They jostle and tease as they each shoot arrows. There's a big, pasty white kid with a blond crewcut, similar to Stick's hair style, and two long-haired kids with skin darker than Stick's well-tanned look.

Stick points. "This is Oliver, Craig, and Joseph." The boys don't turn around.

"Boys." Gloria's voice rings in clear and stern, but not loud.

The boys stop playing and look at us. Stick continues, gesturing at me, "This is Martin."

"Hi, Martin," the boys all chorus before looking at Gloria for approval.

I wave, feeling a bit uncomfortable in the sudden spotlight. "Uh, hi."

A girl on the couch, who has been ignoring everyone from behind her book, peeks out. She has short, black hair and tanned skin like Stick. In fact, she's the only person who looks like him at all. "Hi, Martin," she says.

"That's Margret," Stick says.

Margret goes back to reading her book before I get "Hi, Margret." out of my mouth.

"We're going to go to my room, okay, Gloria?" Stick says. He doesn't move until she gives her approval. Then we walk down a set of stairs on the other side of the foyer.

We enter a rumpus room with toys and a ping-pong table, which has seen better days. Stick opens a door off the hall and leads me into a room with two beds. "I have to share my room with Oliver," he explains.

"That sucks," I say, imagining sharing my room with anyone.

Stick shrugs. "It's not so bad. He worships me, so it makes things go pretty smoothly."

Stick's room has no pictures on the wall. The beds are made, and there are no clothes on the floor. Even the desk is tidy, with everything neatly stacked or placed in a container. It's weird. Really weird.

"So," I say, "you have a big family."

Stick chuckles. "They're not my family. Except for Margret, that is. She's my sister."

"So, your parents are into adoption?"

Stick shakes his head. "This is a foster home."

"Whoa!" a surge of fear jolts through me. I take a half-step back. "What did you do?"

Stick's smile dies away and is quickly replaced with a threatening scowl. "I didn't do *anything*."

"So, how'd you end up here?" I ask, confused.

"My parents are total screw-ups."

I sit down on one of the beds, not sure if it's Stick's or Oliver's, since they both look identical. "No way."

Stick sits across from me. "Yeah. They didn't even show up for court when Margret and I were first removed. Didn't even fight for us or anything. Liked their drugs better."

My stomach drops like when I miss a step and plunge suddenly. "How long have you been here?"

"Me, not that long. Margret's been living here just over a year. I've been to four different homes. I only got here three months ago when a spot opened up. It's taken me that long to finally get back together with Margret."

This information really changes how I look at Stick. The way he acted, I thought he had it all together. Stable family. Good home. Now, it's like I'm meeting him for the first time. "So, do you have to stay here forever?" I ask, trying to take in all this information.

Stick shrugs. "If my parents keep doing what they're doing I might be here until I turn eighteen. But things change all the time. I'm never quite sure what's going on."

"And on your eighteenth birthday . . ."

"I'm gone. Unless Gloria wants to rent me a room. But, I won't be able to stay in the same room as a foster kid, for one thing. And the government stops paying for me, too. So, chances are —"

"You'll get kicked out?"

"Pretty much. At least I can apply for welfare and rent a place, so I can finish grade twelve."

"Holy crap," my brain pounds under the weight of Stick's problems.

"Whatever." Stick shrugs. "That's not what really bugs me."

"What, then?"

His face gets that hard look. Angry. "I hate it when people blame me for being here. I mean, it's not my fault my parents are messed up drug addicts. But, as soon as people hear foster care, they always look at me like I'm the criminal."

I shift uncomfortably. "Yeah, sorry about

that. I didn't know. I guess I've never really thought about it. You know, why kids end up here." I blunder on. "And sorry about the other day too." I'm starting to see how whining about my parents could set Stick off. I have parents to whine about, Stick doesn't.

Stick gets up and waves his hand at me. "Don't worry about it. I was having a bad day anyway. I try to keep things from getting to me. But, it doesn't always work. I'm getting better, though. Parkour helps. It helps a lot. You know, the whole philosophy behind it."

"What?" I ask. "Climb on things?"

Stick laughs so hard he almost chokes. "No. More like, fear is your biggest obstacle."

"Fear? Not mega-high jumps?"

"Fear is what makes me stop in my tracks, get mad, lash out. Fear stops the flow."

"What flow?"

"The flow." Stick waggles his arm in front of him. "You know, from object to object. From place to place. Over, through, and around situations."

"Oh," I nod, still not really getting it. "The *flow*."

"Parkour is about overcoming obstacles quickly, efficiently, and without disruption to your path. It's not only about physical barriers. It's also about mental ones. That's why you have to live it, not just practise it."

"If you say so. How did you get into parkour, anyway?" I ask.

"I used to be kind of self-destructive. I was following the same route as my parents. Things were looking bad. Then, I got this social worker, Dave. He was really into parkour. He explained how it worked. Took me to his gym."

"And it worked?" I ask.

"Well, not right away. But, at least I was too tired from training to get into trouble. Eventually, though, I found my own path. I stopped being scared of all the obstacles my parents, the system, life threw in front of me and learned to move over them, instead of being blocked by them." Stick laughs and waves his hand. "But, hell, I'm not perfect. My temper tantrum the other day kind of proves that."

"Yeah, well." I blush. "It wasn't entirely your fault." I look around at the bare room. "So, you're in foster care. How do you pay for training?"

"Dave makes sure I get funding and he's the one who signs my permission forms. Now, if for some reason he quits being my social worker . . . then there might be an issue."

"You really don't have much control in your life, huh?"

"Only when I'm doing parkour," Stick says. "Parkour can take a bad day and make it great. It can make a great day amazing. You should really try it."

"I'd die."

"Anyone can do it. Really," He smiles. "It might help you figure out how to get along with your dad."

I shake my head. "No way that's going to happen."

"Is he really that bad?" Stick asks.

I shrug. I don't want to make Stick mad again, so I change the subject. "Moviemaking is my thing." I stand up. "Want to see the one of you and your crew? It's finally up."

Stick pumps his fist and gets the laptop up and running. We surf over to his brand-new YouTube channel. He watches the fifteen-minute movie wide-eyed. "That rocks!" he says when it finishes. "You made us look so good."

"You guys are good."

"I love the angles you shoot at. You should totally go to a moviemaking school or some-thing."

I shrug. It actually has never occurred to me to look for a film school. I mean, it's school, right? Then again, that might be the kind of school I could finally get along with.

"So, anyway," I say, "I wanted to talk to you about the idea I had for the last scene of my movie."

"Okay. What?" Stick tips his head to the side and leans his hip on the desk.

I describe the scene to him, finishing with "It has to be somewhere apocalyptic, where the world is crumbling, but still a great place to shoot some decent tricks."

"So, you're talking the brewery," Stick says, eyebrow raised.

"It's the only logical choice."

"If we get caught, I could get kicked out of here."

I bite my lip. "If you don't want to do it."

"I didn't say that," Stick says, his lips forming a crooked smile. "I said, *if* we get caught. So — let's not get caught."

11

CAUGHT

Dad slams the front door, his face demon red. He opens his mouth to make yet another point, spittle flying. He's been making points all the way home from school. At top volume. I can't take much more of it.

"You're a thief!" Dad points his finger in my face.

I want to bite it. I imagine my teeth snapping forward in a tight close-up, like the monster from the *Alien* movie franchise. Jutting out and cleaving his finger in two, blood spurting all over the camera.

Instead, I mutter, "I didn't steal anything."

"Plagiarizing is the same as stealing. Didn't you think your English teacher would notice the majority of that essay came from a student she taught only *last year*?"

I'm going to kill York.

"Then, I had to miss another day of work bailing you out of the office, *again*!"

"You didn't . . ." I trail off. Dad's screaming always ends up lowering my volume.

"What?"

"You didn't bail me out last time. I didn't do anything," I repeat a little louder.

Dad's face goes from red to plum. "I was called in, wasn't I?"

If I were shooting this, I'd have the camera up near the ceiling — pointed down in a medium range, high-angle shot, so the audience could read our body language. I'm crouched, shoes half off. Dad is leaning over me, chin jutting, chest puffed, finger waving like a sword. This is about domination. Dad being right. Me being wrong. Once he thinks he's gotten that through to me, he'll screw off to watch TSN.

I can't wait until he's satisfied.

Dad makes another point — his last one, I hope. "You're lucky I didn't rat you out."

"Huh?" I stand up and kick my shoes onto the mat.

"You think I don't know?" Dad snarls.

Nope, not getting any clearer.

He skewers me with his finger. Right in the chest. "Your teacher says your work is all over the map. One minute it's barely readable, the next it's more of a junior high level. Then, you bring her that piece of plagiarized crap." Dad huffs out a long breath. Runs his hand over what little hair he has. Lifts his lip, sneering. "You've been using your sister."

I'm not sure what to say. If I admit it, Carly might get in trouble. If I deny it, Dad won't believe me. Or worse, he will, and I'll have to live up to Carly's standards of essay writing. I don't think I could pull that off.

"Did you blackmail her into it? Did you con her? Did you offer her money?" Dad asks each question like a machine gun on automatic, three-round bursts. I can almost see the flash of gunpowder lighting up his open mouth. Sparks shooting off his teeth. If I could record this, I'd make it happen with my special effects software.

"I can't believe you, Martin," Dad continues, ranting. "I really can't. Your mom and I have tried to instil some kind of moral compass in you. But, it's like you don't care. You're just out for you. So, why did she do it? Answer me!"

I try to pick a reply that will keep Carly from getting into trouble. And me too, if I can manage it. "She was trying to help me."

"Help you? What? Be lazier than you already are?"

Zoom in on me. My body went rigid. Pan up. Adjust the focus for a close-up. My face turning to steel. Teeth clenched. Extreme close-up. My eyes narrow.

"I'm not lazy!" Inside my chest a paper bag filled with enraged wasps tears open. They burn and sting as they buzz around. I try to say something, anything, to get him to understand how angry he makes me. But, what comes out isn't what I wanted. What comes out is, "I can't read!"

I stand rigid, waiting for his reaction.

Dad eyes me. Gives me a good, long look that starts at my head, goes down to my feet, then back up. "Bullshit," he finally declares.

"Well, I have trouble with it," I correct, stuttering and backtracking. "Reading is hard. Writing too. It's like, I don't know, the words and letters move around on the page."

Dad's face goes from angry to concerned. He scans deep into my eyes. I think he might actually be getting it. That I have a problem. That I've been trying.

"Are you sure you haven't been using drugs?"

I want to slap myself with a double-handed face palm. "No, Dad. I don't do drugs."

"Then, how do words move, huh?"

I shrug.

I don't know how words swap places and letters end up backward. I can't tell him why they seem to wiggle on the page as if they've had too much caffeine. Or why I get motion sick when I read. Maybe I'm mental. Maybe I'm insane. All I know is, I don't have any answers.

After a minute of silence, while I struggle to come up with an explanation, *any* explanation, Dad clamps his lips in a smug smile. "Yeah, I thought so," he says. "So, it's one more lie in a long list of lies." He thumps his hand onto my shoulder, thick fingers squeezing. "Martin, it's simple. All you have to do is buckle down. Stop playing around with that stupid camera and study. Do your work. Take responsibility."

"Why don't you fuck off!" I'm screaming. Fed up. He doesn't care who I am or what's important to me. "There's more to life than grades!"

"God, that article was right," Dad mutters as his scowl goes from parental to vicious. "Give me your camera."

"What?" In my mind the floor opens up and drops me down a long, black shaft. Shot from above, all the audience sees is a speck in the distance disappearing into nothingness. Seconds later, there's a thud.

"Give me your camera."

"Dad, come on," I'm pleading.

"You can have it back when your marks go up."

My marks? Go up? Impossible. "No, Dad. Come on."

He pushes past me slanting toward my room. I dodge in front of him. Throw my body across the doorway, fingers clutched on the door frame.

"Please, Dad. I'll try harder."

"I know you will." Dad grabs my shoulders and pulls me out of the way. "Move."

"But, I've entered this contest. A making movie contest." I blurt, my words coming out backward as they clamber over each other, fighting to be first.

"A making movie contest," Dad sneers.

"SHUT UP! You know what I mean!" I yell, face radiating sudden heat.

"Don't you tell me —"

STUPID

I barrel ahead, pulse quickening. "The contest ends this Friday. I have to get my entry in. I'm not done shooting. I need the camera. Come on." My voice trembles with my final words. Tears blur my vision. Hurriedly I wipe them away. Try to get it together.

"You can have your camera," Dad says.

Hope soars.

"After your marks come up."

And is body slammed right back down. "But, the contest."

"There will be other contests. You can enter those. I'm doing this for your own good." He pulls open my dresser drawers, searching for my camera bag. "Where is it?"

I position myself between him and my closet. "Can't you even try to understand? I've already shot most of the movie. I've done hours of work."

"Work?" Dad says, "You don't know what work is." He pushes past me again, rips open the closet door, and emerges with my two camera bags swinging in his fist.

"Give them back."

"I've already told you how you can get it all back."

"You're not being fair!"

"No, Martin, *you're* not being fair — to yourself. Think about all the hours you've spent making that movie. If you had used that time responsibly this wouldn't be happening." Dad walks to the door.

I lunge. Snatch. Dad pulls the camera bags away. They knock into the wall with a thud. The lenses rattle.

"You're such an asshole!" I shout.

"You want to keep that up?" He glares. Pins me with his look. Vicious is gone, cruel has taken its place. "I'll smash the whole goddamned thing to bits, right now!"

He brings back his arm.

"Fine," I say. "Take them." I turn. Sit down at my desk. Start up my computer. Say nothing more.

My fingers vibrate on the keyboard.

12

SEARCHING

Dad is in the living room. He's been there all night watching sports and playing on his tablet. Mom's out. With four big weddings going off this weekend and one on Friday, she won't be home for hours. Carly is in her room talking to Jamie or Justin or whoever is drooling over her right now. And, me, I'm searching.

Moving down the hall, silent, I get to my target. Turn the doorknob. Open the door quick. Slip in. Pull it shut it behind me. Inside my parent's bedroom. I turn on one of the bedside lamps. My hand knocks into a book. It thuds to the floor.

Crap.

I freeze. Listen. Pray. There's no noise, except the cheer of the crowd coming from the living room TV. I put the book back and start to move.

I try to think like Dad. Attempt to imagine where I would put my camera if I were him. I look in his closet. Top shelf. Nothing but clear storage boxes filled with photos, old drawings, and report cards. Mom is a bit of a hoarder when it comes to childhood memories. Fabric rustling, hangers clinking, the musky scent of my dad's cologne, I push his suits aside and search the dark corners. They're empty, with the exception of a couple of shoe boxes, actually containing shoes. He doesn't even have any skin magazines. Is this what it's like to grow up? Rows of shoes and nothing else? No wonder he hates me. My creativity must burn a hole right through him.

I leave the closet and check his drawers. Everything neat and organized. No camera.

Tension pulls my skin tight, makes my pulse flutter. I try Mom's drawers. She has stuff everywhere. There's even a small tube of sky-blue paint lost in amongst her slacks and my great-grandfather's war medal in with her socks. But, no camera.

I hunt under the bed. Nothing. On the top of the wardrobe. Nothing. Between the dressers. Nothing. I even lift the tablecloth up from Mom's makeup table. Nothing, nothing, nothing.

"Hey, Dad!" I hear Carly say. She sounds loud.

And close.

Crap again.

"Can I show you something — on your tablet? Please?" Carly's voice is sugary sweet — and urgent.

"But, I was going to get . . ." Dad counters.

In my mind I can see Carly, blue eyes gleaming. Willing Dad to do her bidding. Trying to move him away from this room.

How did she know I was in here?

"Please? It will only take a second," she begs.

There's a full-out huff, then, "Fine. But why is it every time you show me something it costs me money?"

"Oh, Daddy. You're so silly!" Carly counters.

I hear them move down the hallway. Back into the living room. I go to turn off the lamp. Hesitate. I've looked everywhere I can think of in this room. Under everything. On top, beside, between, behind *everything*. My camera and lenses are not in here. *So, where are they?* I click off the lamp and escape.

Back in my room I sketch the last panels of the storyboard, mentally searching the house. I've been everywhere. Looked everywhere. I can't find my camera. Under my pencil the final scene at the brewery takes shape. I glance at the clock. I'm supposed to meet Stick in an hour. Sneak out and finish filming. But, with no camera, our plan is undone.

Where is it?

The blur of Stick's eyes as he dashes by emerges from the paper. My door knob turns. Carly slips in. She flops down beside me on the bed.

"Thanks," I say.

She grabs my notebook out of my hand. "No problem. Awesome pictures. You making a new movie?"

I nod. "I was. We were supposed to film the last scene tonight."

"We?" She eyes me. "Is this like the royal we, or have you actually made a friend who isn't imaginary?"

"Stick's real."

A crafty smile plays across Carly's lips. "Is he cute? Does he have a girlfriend?" She leans into my shoulder. "Or is he into guys?"

"Cut it out."

Carly laughs from behind her nail polish, then gets serious. "You should have paid me to write that essay. I don't plagiarize."

"I was broke."

"Well . . . I still would have done it." She

kicks her feet, stubby nose pointed up at the ceiling. "Probably." She looks back at me. "So, what's your movie about?"

"I'm trying to show the way I see the world using parkour."

"You mean that running and jumping stuff?"

"Yeah. The contest ends in a few days, and I still have this last scene to —"

Carly punches my shoulder. "You entered a contest? For real?"

"What?" I say, giving her a playful shove back.

"You never enter contests. You said —"

"It's something new," I say. "I'm trying something new."

"Why don't you tell Dad about it? I'm sure he'd give you back your —"

"I did tell Dad. He couldn't care less."

Carly bites her bottom lip, sucking it into her face. She twirls her sandy hair around her finger. "Maybe he wants . . ." She trails off.

"What?" I ask.

"Maybe he wants you to . . ." Carly stops herself again mid-sentence. Points her face back at the ceiling.

"What?"

"Go away."

"What are you talking about?"

"Mom and Dad are going to send you away."

"Bull."

Carly's pulled some dirty tricks on me, but nothing this mean. And the way she looks, like she's going to cry. It makes me think she might be telling the truth. "Are you sure?"

"I think so." Carly says, leaning her head on my shoulder. "Dad just showed me the boarding school on his tablet. A military one. For kids with ADHD."

"I don't *have* ADHD."

"It doesn't matter. Mom and Dad think you do and so does the doctor."

"That still doesn't prove Dad is trying to get rid of me."

"He showed me some of the school

activities. Joked that I might even like to go there if it weren't just for boys."

I cover my face with my hands. Rub at my eyes. Try to stop this nightmare. "Maybe it's nothing. Maybe he was just looking."

"I don't think so," Carly sighs, "I also heard Mom and Dad talking last week about finding you a different school. One that could help you learn better. I thought they meant another school in Calgary."

"But a boarding school?"

"In Ontario," Carly clarifies.

"Damn."

We sit in silence. Listen to a trapped fly bounce against the window, buzzing fretfully. Outside, purple twilight closes in on the peacock sky. Finally Carly says. "I'll help you study. I'll do your essays. For free even. Maybe if your marks go up —"

I launch my pencil across the room. It clatters off the far wall. The fly buzzes up to the ceiling. "It won't matter."

"But —"

"Dad hates me. Besides, if I don't have my camera, who cares?"

"I do. Please." Carly's eyes are brimming with tears. Real tears, not the fake ones she can spout on demand over the latest spring fashions. "Please, try to stay."

I sigh and wrap my arm around my kid sister. She shakes beside me. Tears glistening as they spill down her cheeks. "Okay. But I need to finish this movie first. Do you have any idea where my camera is?"

Carly looks up at me, wiping her eyes with the back of her hand, a grin shining on her mottled face. "I can find out."

13

DREAMING OF A BETTER TOMORROW

True to her word, Carly comes through. Not half an hour later I'm out my window with my camera bumping my hip in a rhythmic beat. I surge with happiness. Feel like nothing can defeat me. The world is mine. I even laugh out loud, my cackles echoing off the underpass as I jog to the brewery.

Stars prickle the sky, salt crystals on black velvet, dimmed only by the glow of the orange street lamps. The air is warm. A promise of summer around the corner. My hair ripples in the strong chinook wind. It's going to be good shooting tonight. I can't wait.

Stick meets me by the train tracks, and together we break in, a reverse of our original great escape. I clamber up the old loading dock frame, using it as a ladder. I'm scrambling, slipping and groping over the inclined metal siding as I climb onto the roof. Stick takes it all at a run.

We both gaze across the expanse, looking for the perfect location. Silently, Stick points. I nod, take my camera out of its bag, and follow him, doing a bit of filming as I go. The moon is bright in the sky. Big and plump, shining down like a spotlight on us. We don't even need flashlights. The rooftop is covered with small, square buildings of different sizes. And some of those have one or two other smaller buildings on them. I point to one of the singletons. Then, point to another twelve feet away. It's more squat by a good two or three feet. I think Stick can make it.

He nods and heads for the ladder. I position myself below the gap. Moon overhead, streaks of fast-moving cloud racing across its face.

Above I can see Stick stretching out. Squatting. Warming up. I know he ran here, but this is a pretty big gap. He has to be sure. He looks over the edge. Peers at his landing zone. Gives me the thumbs-up and backs up out of sight. I hit record. The little red light starts flashing.

Then, he's running. Legs pumping hard, he hits his final step with power, chest pushed out, arms flung forward. His legs come up in a tuck before his arms swing behind him like wings, and he lands on the other roof, rolling over his shoulder with barely a sound. Next thing I know, he's crouching behind me, not having used the ladder at all.

"So, how'd it look?" Stick whispers.

I play the video back. He's a shadow puppet on the white moon. His grey jogging pants and yellow T-shirt only adding flashes of accent, like speed lines in an anime. Stick whistles softly. "Wow!"

He points farther along the roof. "I have an idea," he says.

I follow him to another low building where he sets me up on a ladder. Camera peeking over the roof.

"Shoot from here," he orders. "Let's see how it turns out."

He takes off, and it's a few minutes before I see him again, leaping onto a building across from mine. He raises his arm, points out his path — a U-shape that takes him up three levels, across a wall, back down two levels, then to me. I focus, hit record, and raise my arm.

Stick starts running. He leaps high in the air, somersaulting before he reaches the ground. Runs. Hits the wall with one foot, arms raised above his head in a crane jump, touching down on the roof with the other foot. Rolls over his shoulder. Runs again. Leaps. Grabs the top of the next wall with both hands, feet tucked up underneath. Then, he jumps, landing with his feet between his hands on the top. Backflips. Lands in the same spot, right on the edge. Front flips and runs, doing a side flip before flying up another level, jumping and twisting his body at the top, and landing in a crouch facing the opposite direction. He front flips in a 180-degree corkscrew to turn around.

From there he runs right for the wall, jumping up and catching the edge with his hands in a perfect cat jump. Then, his feet moving quickly up the wall, Stick precision jumps onto the next set of buildings, doing a half-turn in the air. He lands in a crouch, runs, and dive rolls down to the next level, landing again in a crouch. From there he pushes into another sideways jump and runs straight off the edge, landing on the building I'm shooting from. He does a side flip, landing it at a run — straight at me. I do my best to keep the camera trained on him, even though I'm flinching inside. His speed isn't letting up. He gets bigger and bigger on the camera's screen until he shoulder rolls and stops with his face an inch away from the lens, grinning like a maniac. I hit the stop button. Let out the breath trapped in my chest as Stick leaps over me.

I stand frozen in place. Stick waits by the bottom of the ladder, arms crossed, looking pretty pleased with himself.

"So?" he asks.

"Let's see," I say, shaking myself out of my trance and climbing down.

We both watch. I'm hoping my focus held. It all happened so fast. But, it looks good. Man, it looks better than good; it's amazing. I can't believe I shot it.

I decide to have Stick hold the camera again while he flips, aiming it at the moon. Then, we shoot a couple of clips where he's scaling broken bricks.

"What else?" Stick asks.

"How high can you get?"

Stick looks around, hands on his hips.

Watching him, I hit record. He looks so strong, brave, like nothing can stop him. I'm always being eaten up by guilt, panic, depression, anger. I feel like my problems throw one wall after another in my face. Maybe if I had Stick's philosophy I could be like him. Fix my world. Overcome my dad and his great ideas. Then again, maybe not. Military school seems pretty unfixable.

Stick juts his chin at the towering sign at the edge of the building, announcing the storage facility. "I could climb that."

I tip my head up and consider the possibilities. "Could you stand on the top and look like you just went up there to, you know . . ." I'm struggling to find the right word.

"Dream?" Stick offers.

"Yeah," I say. "Dream."

"I can do that," Stick replies and starts running.

I head off to find a place to shoot from. I want to be far enough away to show how high up he is. I switch over to my telephoto lens.

Stick scales the huge sign from the inside, using the scaffolding that makes up the frame. Once up, he stands tall, on the very top, body buffeted by the strong wind that's only picking up speed. He looks into the distance, clothes flapping furiously. It's perfect. I film him for a good long time, zooming in on Stick's face pointed up at the moon.

Finally I turn off the camera, put it back in its bag, and walk over to Stick. He's still up on the sign, looking out, dreaming of a better tomorrow.

"I'm done," I call up.

"Great," he yells back. "Come up here. The view is amazing." He sits on the sign, like it's nothing.

I look up. The sign is at least thirty feet tall with large wooden beams running at a forty-five-degree angle securing it to the building. It buffers in the wind, creaking like a haunted house. Inside, I shake with fear. *I wonder if Stick feels like that. Inside.* If he does, he chooses to ignore it and lives the way he wants. I would love to be able to do that. To leave my fear behind.

Steeling myself I slip inside, grab the metal scaffolding, and haul myself up, higher and higher. Not looking down. Not breathing. Just thinking about the next step, the next handhold. Trying to ignore the wind thumping on the metal panels of the sign like a giant's hammering fist. Finally I'm swinging my leg over the top bar and sitting beside Stick.

And the view *is* amazing.

"Makes it worth it, right?" Stick says, nudging me.

I grip the edges of the sign *hard*. It sways beneath me. But, I nod all the same. "This is what you see when you do parkour?"

"Sometimes." Stick keeps his eyes on the horizon. Where the speckled city lights meet up with black, star-clustered sky. "Sometimes, when things aren't going well. When the news is bad, or I've had a rough day, I climb as high as I can go and sit. It quiets all the chatter in my head, you know?"

"I do now," I breathe.

"Hey!" The security guard, far below, waves his flashlight at us. "Get down from there. I'm calling the cops."

"Time to bolt." Stick says, he swings his

leg over the edge and bounces down the scaffolding to the roof.

I swing my legs over and, lying on my stomach, feel with my toes for an edge. Stick is pacing.

"We have to go. I can't get caught," he says.

Feet finally touching something I can climb, I scramble down, and we run. The security guard is down on the ground, monitoring our escape route. "Come on," Stick says, and turns the opposite direction, racing along the roof and up a ladder to a low building. He's already leaping over a five-foot gap to another low roof by the time I get up. I rush to follow. He lands smoothly, like a cat. I land hard, jarring my knees and rattling my teeth, cradling my camera bag in one arm like a football. Stick is already leaping again, jumping back down to the main roof. I groan and follow, landing with softer knees this time and not hurting myself as badly. The security guard follows on the ground. Yelling curses every time he catches a glimpse of us. We keep running, trying to stay ahead of him. Hoping to get down before he cuts us off again. It's then that I see where Stick is leading. The place I came up last time.

The pipes.

Skidding to a halt at the edge I peer down, looking for the guard and checking out the lay of the land. It looks even more dangerous than when I came up it a week and a half ago, and it didn't look all that safe before. The black, spongy roof of the building below is a good fifteen feet down and over a three-foot gap.

"We're not going to jump onto that, are we?"

"Have to," Stick says, "but not from up here. You grab onto that big, black pipe over there. The one you came up last time." He points. "Slide down it and get as close to the roof as you can. Bend your knees when you land and use the balls of your feet."

"You coming too?" I ask.

Stick shakes his head and jumps over the edge of the building, disappearing. I run over and look down, fearing the worst. He's landed on the piece of aluminum sticking out of the wall. From there he swings over to the small horizontal pipes, dangling, before leaping the last ten feet, spinning in a 180-degree turn, and rolling over his shoulder as he hits the roof. "Your turn."

"I hate you!" I yell down.

"Go. The big pipe."

I run over to the pipe, chanting, "Don't be afraid. Don't be afraid," but it doesn't help.

I sit on the edge of the building, grab the pipe, and wrap my arms around it. As soon as I push off, my hands begin to slip. I grip tighter, plant my feet on the wall, and try to control myself. The pipe creaks. My hands slip again. Then, there's a shudder and a screech. Dust rains down all around me reeking of rancid oil and mouse droppings. A crack snaps through the air, and the whole pipe comes loose from the building. Nightmare slow, the whole thing starts swinging away from the wall. I try to grab at the brick with my toes, but, in seconds, it's too far away.

"Help!" I yell. I'm moving away from the roof, out into open space.

"Jump!" Stick orders. "Hurry."

I wrap the camera bag in one arm and I fling myself from the pipe. My attempt at following Stick's directions to land softly on the balls of my feet doesn't work. I smash into the roof. My knees collapse and slam into my jaw. My left foot lands hard on the heel. My right foot breaks through the rotting boards. Shards of wood spear my ankle with laser-like pain. Warm blood fills my shoe. I'm terrified to look down.

Stick runs over. "Oh, God! Don't move."

Sirens howl in the distance. I want to howl too. Frustration and fear, pain and panic throw my heartbeat and breathing into overdrive. I yank on my leg. Agony blasts through it. I almost throw up. "I can't get it out," I gasp, the cold of shock washing over me.

"You need an ambulance," Stick says. He looks up. "That jump was way too high. This roof . . ." His head falls to his chest. "Sorry."

The sirens get louder. There's a screech of brakes.

Pain shoots up my leg again as I accidentally

shift. My knees throb. Lip swells. But this situation is bigger than me and my problems. I clench my teeth. Fight to get my fear and panic under control. "I don't want you to get blamed for this," I say to Stick.

"But —"

"It was my idea. My movie. And —" I hold out the camera. "I need you to get this to safety. If my dad catches me with it, it's gone. Probably forever. Please."

I know Stick is valiant. If this were medieval times he'd be a knight. I have to get him out of here. He doesn't deserve what's coming.

Stick nods, takes my camera bag, and pulls the strap over his head, wrapping an arm around it tight. "Okay. Good luck."

A car doors slams. Voices echo off the buildings.

"You too," I say. "Now go."

Stick jumps from the building. I don't even hear his shoes on the concrete as he races to freedom.

14

HARD CHOICES

"Where is it?" Dad screams. His coat is still on from the hospital. He didn't even stop at the door before racing past me to check his precious hiding spot. The lens bag was there; the camera, not so much.

I ignore him, struggling as I try to take off the shoe from my good foot while leaning on my crutches. My right foot is bandaged up, the ankle stitched and scraped. It could have been worse. Injury-wise, anyway. At least I got some nice pain killers. Now I can see why York does a booming business in this stuff.

"Where is it?" Dad shouts again, getting right in my face.

"Where's what?" I say, like I have no idea.

"Where. Is. Your. Camera?" He bites each word, snapping his teeth in my face.

"I don't have it." I glance toward the living room. "Where's Mom?" I figured she'd be here to meet me since she didn't come to the hospital.

"I told her to stay at work. I'm dealing with this," Dad declares.

"Great," I mutter.

I finally get my shoe off and start to hobble toward my room, but Dad grabs my shoulder, nearly throwing me off balance.

"You're paying that trespassing fine, you know," he growls.

I shrug. Two thousand dollars, plus whatever damages the brewery wants to charge me with. It's better than a criminal record, but I have no idea where I'm going to get that kind of money.

Dad continues. "The police said there were two of you."

I still don't say anything.

"The other guy has your camera, right?"

I shrug again.

"Does he?" Dad's voice gets louder.

"Why do you care so much?" I sneer.

Dad pokes his finger in my face. God, I hate that. I want to punch him every time he does it.

"You want to know why I care?" he rants. "Because every time you leave with that camera, your attitude goes in the toilet."

My attitude?

"You get defiant. You break rules."

"I don't break rules because of my camera," I say.

Dad looks smug. "So, you just break rules."

"Yeah," I pause. "I mean, no. I mean. Hell, I'm just a normal teenager!"

"I don't call trespassing normal. Or flunking every class you take. Or paying your little sister to do your school work. You've fallen into a bad place, Martin, and I'm going to pull you out, even if it means calling in the big guns."

I think of what Carly said about Dad wanting to ship me to a military boarding school for ADHD boys. "Are you planning on sending me away?" I ask.

"Who told you that?" Dad looks shocked, caught off guard.

"Are you?" I persist.

"Mr. Jefferson recommended a school that might help. One his nephew went to. Your mom and I have been looking into it," Dad replies.

"Mom wants me gone too?"

"We don't want you gone, Martin. We want to help you."

"But, you're sending me away."

"This place can deal with your issues."

"I don't have issues!" I scream.

"You can't pass a test!"

"So, what? Einstein couldn't pass a test."

"Einstein isn't my son!" Dad switches gears. "The school is really nice. It has great activities. They can even get you off your medication."

"Good!" I snap. "Because I don't have ADHD."

"Well, you have something!" Dad shouts, starting to lose it again. "ADHD, idiot's disorder, general stupidity. I don't care what the hell you call it, you need to be fixed! Okay?" He pauses. Runs his hand through what's left of his hair. "Look. It's obvious." He ticks the points off on his fingers. "You're easily distracted. You refuse to engage in things that don't interest you —"

"Yeah? Well, do you?" I interrupt. "You do everything you can to screw with my movie-making."

"Right," Dad says, smirking like I've walked right into his trap. "So, where is the camera?"

Crap. *How did I end up on the game show Dig Your Own Grave?* I shut my mouth. Say nothing.

"Fine." Dad moves past me and heads for my room, yanking open the door and banging it against the wall. "Two can play this game."

I hobble after him.

By the time I get to my room Dad has my laptop unplugged. "You won't give me the camera. You don't get your computer. Or your phone." He puts out his hand, palm pointed up. "Hand it over."

I stand there. Brain buzzing. Pulse galloping. "Seriously?"

"Now."

In a microsecond I think of my options. My phone I can lose. My laptop has ninety per cent of my movie on it. Most of it edited. If that goes, so does any chance of entering the contest. Or putting up more parkour videos. Or making any movies at all. Giving up my camera, well, that would suck. Big time. And losing it right now would mean giving up the footage we shot tonight.

I chew my lip. Think harder. If I had my laptop I could probably finish the movie without that last scene. I mean I have a lot of footage on the computer already. And I might even be able to get the memory card from the camera before handing it over. Or Carly could snag it.

I scowl. Let my mind branch out to other possible solutions. I guess if I let my camera go I could borrow Carly's point-and-shoot for a while. Or even use my phone's camera. It's decent. Hell, I can film with my Nintendo 3DS if I get really desperate. It's not ideal. It's not what I want to work with. But, at this point, with the contest deadline only days away, it's probably better than losing the laptop.

My choice made out of all my crappy options, I finally say, "I'll take you to the camera."

I only hope Stick understands.

15

DAMAGE CONTROL

We're driving. Silent. Streetlights making white lines over the interior of the car. I'm sick with guilt at how weak I am. I know this is going to get Stick in trouble.

I should have let Dad take the computer.

"You made the right choice," Dad says.

I look out the window, watching his reflection. Hating him.

"You'll like this school," he goes on, trying to sound upbeat.

I don't reply.

"They do all kinds of stuff there, rock climbing, mountain biking, sports." He glances over at me. "The uniforms are nice."

I won't look at him. Not directly.

"They have small classes, too. Maybe they can teach you something. Make you less, you know, stupid."

"Stop calling me stupid!" It's out of my mouth before I realize.

Dad's face reddens under my glare. "Maybe if you made better choices —" he says.

"My choices are fine."

"Really?"

"Yeah, really." I turn and look out the window again.

It's a while before Dad asks, "So, who is this . . . What did you call him, Stick?"

"My friend."

"And do his parents know where he was tonight?"

I shrug. "Probably not. He doesn't live with his parents."

"Really? What is he? A runaway?"

"No. He lives in a foster home."

Dad's concern makes his forehead wrinkle.

"What did he do?"

"Nothing, Dad! Don't be stupid."

"Watch your tone!" Dad commands.

Figures. He can call me stupid, but I'm not allowed use the word on him.

"So this, Stick . . . is that his real name?"

I'm so done with this conversation that I'm actually relieved when we pull up in front of the house. Dad gets out first and grabs my crutches from the trunk, handing them to me. I hobble behind him to the door. He rings the doorbell. Gloria answers. She frowns until she sees me and then a smile grows on her face. "Hi, Martin."

My dad introduces himself. I see his head bob as he tries to see beyond Gloria, into the house. He's probably expecting some kind of jail set-up or something. He'll be disappointed. Gloria has a really nice house.

She invites us in and asks, "What can I do for you?"

Dad clears his throat and pulls himself straight. "I'm sorry to tell you this, but the boy you call, Stick," Dad glances at me, making sure he got the name right, "has my son's camera. I would appreciate if he would give it back," Dad finishes.

Gloria's face goes hard. Like stone.

I fly into panicked damage control. "Stick didn't steal anything. I gave him the camera. He was holding onto it for me. As a favour. Really. I promise. My dad's just —"

Gloria holds up her hand, stopping me cold. "Alan," she calls. Stick appears seconds later. I can tell by his pinched eyebrows that he's scared. I try to tell him I'm sorry without talking. Show him somehow. But, I'm not sure it gets through.

"Alan, do you have Martin's camera?"

Stick nods.

"Please go and get it, then." Gloria talks in no-nonsense, clipped sentences.

Stick turns and goes downstairs to his room, returning with my camera bag moments later. He hands the bag to Gloria, who gives it to my dad.

Dad pulls the camera out of the bag, then opens up the memory card slot and peers inside. "So, it's all here. I didn't figure you'd be that honest."

"And why would that be?" Gloria asks.

"He was trespassing with my son tonight. In fact, it was probably his idea, given his," Dad glances around before looking directly at Gloria once more, "upbringing. If you know what I mean."

"You were trespassing? Is this true?" Gloria asks Stick.

Stick starts to answer, but I speak up. "It wasn't his fault. None of it was. Stick tried to talk me out of it. Really. He was trying to stop me. He didn't even go on the property. It was all —"

Stick stops my avalanche of words. "I was helping Martin film his movie. He's entering a contest and wanted some stunt work. We went to the old brewery and broke in. I took his camera when he hurt his ankle to make sure it didn't get taken away." Stick bows his head. Stands resigned. "I'm sorry. I shouldn't have done it. I wasn't trying to cause trouble."

Gloria nods.

Dad turns on the camera. "Well, that's an interesting story. Still, there's no reason either one of you should benefit from what you've done tonight." He hits the trash button twice. The screen asks him if he would like to delete all.

I hold my breath.

His thumb moves over the selection button and presses down.

All the flips and jumps and awesome climbs. Stick standing on top of the sign like he owned the world. The end to my movie. Everything is —

Erased.

16

THE END

I didn't sleep last night. Couldn't pay attention in school today. My ankle aches. My brain is on standby. And now, with the clock ticking over to seven-thirty p.m., I've been looking at the same damn video clips for well over three hours.

And nothing is coming together.

The movie is pretty much done. My voice-over speech, written and recorded by flashlight at two in the morning, finished. All the editing, music, and transitions, complete. The only thing missing is the end. That final scene.

I've been searching through all my clips, trying to find just the right thing. Scenes that might replace the stuff my dad deleted. And every time I think I have something, it doesn't work. It's just not right.

I don't even want to do this anymore.

I pull my good foot up on my chair and wrap my arms around my knee. Bruised chin resting on my jeans. Watching the screen. Stick leaps up, grabbing onto the bridge at Century Gardens. He pulls himself up like it's nothing. Like gravity is only a theory, and not a very good one at that. Soon the screen is overlaid with images from my mind. Memories of last night. Of climbing the inside of that sign. The wind howling. Metal banging. Of being terrified, but making it anyway. Sitting way up in the air, next to Stick, looking out at all the city lights, each one a possibility.

That's a high York could never sell. I wish I was there now. Instead of here. With Dad. The guy who deleted my dreams and then took my camera.

I look up at the calendar. Test tomorrow in English. We're done tearing *To Kill a Mockingbird* apart. It's time to see if we learned anything. I know I should study. I promised Carly. But what's the point? Dad's made up his mind, and Mom, she's going along with it. Why bust my balls on something that won't make any difference. Still, I reach into my backpack. Grab my binder. Flip to my cryptic notes.

I can at least try. For Carly.

Half an hour later a ping sounds from my computer. I click over to Facebook. It's Stick messaging me. He's written, "I had to break it into bits, but it's all there. Might take a few messages to get it to you."

Below his message I see a video clip. I click it and up comes Stick jumping over me, the moon behind him. Our footage! I download it and watch, as over the next hour clip after clip comes through.

Finally Stick writes: "That's the last of it."

I type, "That's amazing. How'd you get it?"

Stick returns, "Downloaded it as soon as I got home. Figured your old man would show up sooner or later. Path of least resistance, right? You grounded?"

"No." I type, careful to keep the words and letters in order. "Just my camera and lenses. Dad wants to send me away to military school."

"You're kidding," Stick replies.

I don't want to talk to Stick too much about my family issues. He's so sensitive. Besides, there's been a question bugging me all day and I need to know. "Do you still have a home?"

I hold my breath waiting as the status of the comment switches to read, then announces that Stick is typing. Finally he replies, "I had a long talk with Gloria last night. Told her everything. She said she didn't like what I had done, but she knew I was a good kid. Said I could stay if I promised to avoid poorly maintained heritage sites."

I sit back and laugh. "That's good news," I type.

"Three days until the contest deadline," Stick writes. "You gonna make it?"

"I will now," I reply. "Thanks."

"No problem. Thanks for the adventure."

I close Facebook and finish reading my English notes. A promise is a promise. Then I get to work on the remainder of the movie. Three days to make this the best thing the judges will ever see. It's going to be amazing. It's going to win. And when it does, I'm going to rub it right in Dad's face. Maybe then he'll see I'm not stupid and won't send me away. Maybe he'll even be proud, instead of embarrassed.

17

AND THE WINNER IS . . .

"Think it's up yet?"

We're all sitting in the lobby of the Central Library, hunched over Stick's phone. I've been filming the guys over at Olympic Plaza using my 3DS game. It's crappy as far as what I'm used to, but it's better than nothing. Besides, it gives me the opportunity to make some 3-D films. Which is kind of sweet. On the plus side, I've managed to ditch the crutches. I can now get around with a limp, my ankle almost healed after two weeks of physiotherapy and antibiotics.

"It wasn't up an hour ago." Stick shrugs.

"But, they said the results would be released

today," Jovy puts in. "You're going to win. I know it. That film was amazing."

"Thanks," I grin.

"We have a winner!" Stick announces pouring over his phone's screen. "Let's see. First place —"

I hold my breath. Wait for him to say my name.

Stick frowns. "Amala Dahwan. What the hell?"

"Let me see that." I snatch the phone out of his hand. Look at the website. First place Amala Dahwan. Second place Zaid Al-Asadi. Third place Kristen Stephenson. Runners-up: me, Kendal Collins, and Sati Massari.

I pass the phone back to Stick. Look down at the table, face burning. Focus on the crumpled wrapper from a straw. Extreme close-up. Every fibre revealed.

"Sorry, man," Stick says, laying his hand on my shoulder. "I thought your movie kicked butt."

The rest of the crew agrees.

Inside I'm burning. Flames licking my

stomach. Eating away the flesh. "Play it," I say. "Let's see this winner." Stick looks worried. "You sure?"

"Yeah." He taps his screen, and the video loads. A few seconds later it starts playing. "Hi," says the smiling girl in her bedroom, "I'm Amala Dahwan and I'm all about volunteering. Let me show you my Calgary." Her hand reaches for the camera. The image shakes, then turns off. Next shot is of Amala as she packs white bread into bags at the food bank. Her voice-over is murky, and she hasn't cut the background sound on the video at all. She talks about how she likes to help the needy on a local and international level. The next shot is of her sitting at a table in her high- school hallway, handing out pamphlets and selling some kind of trinket. Again the background noise is battling with her voice-over. The camera shakes as someone trips over the tripod. I hear shouting off screen.

Stick hits the stop button well before the end. "Wow. That sucked."

"Yeah," James says. "That was nowhere

near as good as your movie."

I don't say anything. Go back to staring at the straw wrapper. Stick must make some kind of motion because his crew, as a unit, tells me my movie should have won, says goodbye, and takes off.

Stick stays. Quiet. I don't say anything, either. All I can think of is how I always fail, no matter how hard I try. I can work my butt off. I can study all night long. It doesn't matter. Math, English, Social Studies, sports, moviemaking, I suck at it all.

"I shouldn't have even tried," I blurt.

"So, the judges were looking for something else. Whatever."

"Whatever?" My eyebrow juts up. "I lost."

"Yeah, to a girl who doesn't trespass. Who doesn't climb a thirty-foot sign in a chinook wind to look at the scenery. Who made a crappy movie with a decent message — which you could barely hear."

"And I still lost to her. So, what does that make my movie? Huh? More crappy?"

"No." Stick gets his face down, so he can look me in the eyes. "It makes the judges crappy."

"Or maybe I just suck."

"Hey," Stick laughs, trying to break the tension. "You saw our footage before you showed up. It was awful. Remember? We didn't know what we were doing. You made us look good. Really good. Everyone thinks so. Our channel has over a thousand hits already. The only reason that girl won is because she volunteers, not because she can make a movie."

"Maybe," I say. "Or maybe I'm too *stupid* to do anything."

And maybe my dad is right.

I stand up. Grab my hoodie, and limp toward the exit. "I have to get home. I need to waste some time trying to do my Social Studies homework, so I can fail at that too. See you around."

Stick waves his hand. He looks upset. But, I don't care. I hate losing. I hate being stupid. I wish I could do something about it, but I can't. I doubt even Dad's military school will help. I'll probably fail at that too.

18

SIXTY OR MORE

I finish up the last of my Social Studies homework, trying to use the words in the text-book to answer the questions. Trying to get a mark above fifty. I wish Carly was home. She could at least tell me if I was on the right track. Half the time I think I know what I'm talking about, but when I read the question again, everything seems wrong.

I hate my stupid brain.

I've spent two hours on this supposed "quick and easy" assignment. Nothing is ever quick and easy. I type the last word in and send the whole thing to the printer. Done.

English homework is next, but I need a break. Opening YouTube I look for videos on movie-making. It's what I do when I don't want to do anything. Watch other people make movies.

Sparks of anxiety and sadness shoot through me again. I can't believe I lost.

Loser. Useless. Stupid.

The guy on the screen talks about how to edit an action scene. I try to pay attention, but my thoughts keep shooting back to Stick's phone. Runner-up. I guess I'm just delusional. I think I'm good at this stuff when, really, all evidence points in the opposite direction.

"When recording, make sure to look for cut-aways. They always make great edit points," the guy on the screen says. I watch until the video ends. Then, I go searching for more videos. Ones I haven't seen a million times. I come across a weird one by GIFTS Films. It's about a kid who ends up at a really strange film school. It makes me laugh. I start to feel better. After a couple of episodes I decide to see if this place is real. It looks like it was shot at an actual film school. Turns out GIFTS stands for Gulf Islands Film and Television School located in British Columbia, a residential summer camp for young filmmakers. A place for kids like me.

The information hits me in a physical and emotional wave. My throat closes up. The beginnings of a sob hiccup in my chest. My vision blurs. I pull my arm across my eyes. Blink. Try to get a grip on myself. But, the more I read, the more my chest tightens. A crazy longing hits my entire body. It's like I've been looking for something like this, people like me, all this time, then BAM, when I'm feeling my worst — there they are.

I gulp down another hiccupped sniffle.

I wish Dad would send me there, instead of military school.

And the more I think of the ADHD school for troubled boys with its early mornings, marching, and uniforms, the more I yearn for a place like GIFTS. *But, how can I get him to send me?* I can't give him what he wants.

Good grades and the right attitude.

Or can I?

I pick up my social studies binder from my desk and flip through it. I did get that sixty-four per cent on a test not too long ago. If I could keep getting help from Carly and the teacher, I should be able to find a way to pull my grades up at least that high. Sixty per cent. That has to be good enough.

I storm out of my room, fly down the hall, and practically smash heads with my dad as I enter the living room. He's gotten up to get a beer. Mom is knitting in her chair, finally taking a night off. Hockey plays on the TV.

"I'll make you a deal!" I yell in Dad's face.

He pushes me back. Hand flat on my chest, putting some space between us. "What kind of deal?"

"If I get sixty per cent or more on all my finals, I don't have to go to military school, and you send me to summer film camp, instead."

Dad narrows his eyes. "Seventy."

"Seventy?" Mom gasps. "That's a bit steep."

"It's a minimum pass at all universities and trade schools," Dad reasons. "Seventy and you have a deal. At least about the military school."

I set my jaw. Glare. I can work on the film school after. Not being sent away is halfway to what I want. "Fine. Seventy and no military school."

"On all your tests," Dad repeats.

"No problem." I turn away. Speed walk back to my room. Slam my door. Slide down it to the floor.

Seventy. Damn. I wasn't even sure how I was going to make it to sixty.

19

PARKOUR IT IS

I get to Stick's house at eight o'clock, as planned. I'm here to show Stick the finished video I shot at the gym he trains at — Breathe Parkour. One of the coaches lent me his sweet Nikon for the job. I want Stick's go-ahead before I burn the finished disk.

It's been difficult to squeeze filmmaking into my intense study schedule. Even harder to maintain the schedule when my marks have only shot up by about four per cent. Getting fifty eights instead of fifty fours isn't enough to keep me out of military school. To say I'm frustrated would be an understatement. I just can't figure out where I'm going wrong.

I plug my thumb drive into Stick's laptop and play the video.

"Man, are you good." Stick grins in that wide way of his. "I love the way you made the gym look and how you magically turn one person into someone else. It's insane."

"That's called a matched cut, not magic," I explain.

"It's still sweet," Stick says. "Hey, Gloria finally saw your video on the contest website. She said it was the best explanation of dyslexia she's ever seen."

I frown. "Dyslexia? What are you talking about? I don't have that."

"You sure?" Stick says. "Gloria seemed to think you were describing it."

I frown. "Isn't that when words go upside down or backward? I've never had that happen." Stick laughs. "I've seen you write letters backward. You know d's and b's."

"But, that's not a whole word. I think it pretty much has to be the entire thing. Right?"

Stick shrugs. "Let's find out." He types dyslexia into the Google search engine and *Dyslexia Test* comes up as a suggestion. "Want to try?" he asks.

"Sure," I reply. "But it's going to say I don't have it."

Stick clicks over to a link and starts asking me questions. "Okay, number one," he reads, ready to click yes, no, or not sure. "Do you have trouble remembering names?"

I think about it. I can always picture people. Even people I've met years and years ago. But, remember names? I have trouble with that. Hell, I've even forgotten my own dad's name a couple of times. "Sometimes," I say.

"There is no sometimes," Stick says. "Yes or no."

"Yes, then."

"Next question. Is it hard to read unfamiliar words?"

"Yeah, of course. If you haven't seen a word before it would be hard to read it, right?"

Stick goes to say something, then shuts his

mouth. He clicks, yes. "Moving on. Do you have trouble spelling short words you know well?"

"I have trouble spelling *all* words."

Stick clicks yes. "Does reading make you tired quickly?"

I didn't know any of these things were part of dyslexia. "Yes."

"When you read, do words move, get blurry, or hard to focus on?"

"Yeah. Words move around all the time."

Stick looks away from the computer screen and straight at me. "How?"

"I don't know. Match cut magic?"

Stick laughs. "Never mind. Let's just finish this." He goes through the rest of the questions. I answer yes to every single one of them, except the question about maintaining concentration. I'm pretty good at that when I'm working on moviemaking. Even homework, I can sit down and study. In the end, I have a score of 220.

"What does that mean?" I ask.

Stick scrolls down. "Anything above a 150 means you have a very strong possibility of dyslexia. Gloria was right."

Dyslexia, wow. "So, what is it?"

Stick goes to YouTube and finds a twelve-minute documentary. It turns out it has to do with language, reading and writing, connecting letters and sounds, figuring out right and left, and orienting. We also learn that dyslexics think in pictures more than words, are highly original, and have vivid imaginations. We end up watching a few more videos, and one thing keeps coming up; a lot of dyslexics are filmmakers.

"I think we've found your people." Stick says.

"I'm dyslexic, not stupid," I say.

"I've never thought you were stupid," Stick frowns.

"My dad calls me that all the time."

"What?" Stick looks shocked. "No wonder you don't like him."

"That's not the worst part." I tell Stick

about the bargain with my dad.

"Seventy per cent, huh?"

"Yeah, but it's not going to happen. I mean, I've been trying really hard to pull my marks up and I'm not making any progress. All of the techniques the teachers tell me to try don't seem to work."

"Well, if there's one thing I've learned from parkour, it's that you have to find your own path. What works for most students might not work for dyslexics. You have to find your way of doing things and go from there."

"So, how do I do that?"

"Start with the basics. That's what we do in parkour."

I raise my eyebrow. "Does everything relate to parkour?"

"Pretty much. Here." Stick points to a website he's brought up. "Beating dyslexia." He clicks on a link. "Okay, rapid intervention. Here's what you need to do. Learn phonics, practise spelling, read out loud, convergence training —"

"Convergence who?" I ask.

Stick clicks on it. "It says you have to focus on the tip of a pen until you train your eyes not to dart around. Evidently that's what makes the letters and words move — or it's part of the problem, anyway."

"How do you read so fast?" I ask, watching Stick absorb the website.

"I'm not dyslexic. Anyway, look, they have this tool up here. It can read the website for you if you want to look at it later. I'll break it down for you right now."

"Okay."

"Hey, perfect." Stick beams.

"What?"

"One of the ways to get your eyes to stay still is to do core exercises."

"What does my core have to do with my eyes?" I ask.

"No idea, but you know what the best core exercise in the world is?"

"Parkour?" I answer, grimacing.

"Parkour." Stick nods.

"I told you I just film parkour. I don't —"

Stick eyes me seriously. "You want to go to military school?"

"No."

"Then . . ."

I bow my head. "Parkour it is."

I might not survive long enough for Dad to ship me off.

20

TRAINING

Three weeks later, and every muscle group hurts. My arms ache and my gut is screaming, but Stick still won't let up.

"Keep going!" he commands. "It's twenty more feet. Twenty feet is nothing. You can do this!"

He has me, runners on the wall, hands on the railing, nothing in between but a five-foot drop. I have to hold my butt cheeks tight, squeeze my abs, and in a semi-coordinated fashion, move my hands and feet sideways a few inches at a time. A bead of sweat drops from my forehead and splashes on the concrete below. I'm about to follow it.

"I see you!" Stick yells, practically in my ear. "You're thinking of quitting, aren't you? You want to go to military school?"

Military school has to be easier than this.

I finish, finally, dropping my feet onto the bottom rung and crawling over to safety. Every part of me is on fire. I wobble to our backpacks and grab a drink. "I hate you," I say.

Stick grins wide. "You'll love me once the girls start noticing your abs. You coming to the gym tonight?"

I nod. "Yeah, probably. It depends on how much studying I get done at lunch."

"Cool, see you then."

Stick takes off to catch the bus, the sun finally getting warm and golden in the sky. I leave for mine, thinking of what I've been through lately.

In the past three weeks I've attempted every dyslexia-controlling technique I can find and then some. Core training with Stick. Eye training by staring at the tip of a pen for five minutes at a time, three times a day. I've isolated words on the printed page using a piece of paper at the top and bottom of what I read. I've downloaded apps that turn computer text into the spoken word. I've found a special font called OpenDyslexic, specifically designed to keep the words from moving around as much. I use ear plugs in class to keep from getting muddled up by other people's talking while I'm doing my work. I've even started recording the teachers in class. That way I can replay their lectures and take proper notes. It also helps when I don't understand what they've said. I just hit pause and look it up online or in my textbook.

Then, there's reading, spelling, and phonics.

Stick is all about hard work; overcoming your weaknesses; and train, train, train. It's a big part of his parkour philosophy, which he seems to spout any chance he gets. Since I have trouble reading, he has me telling bedtime stories four times a week (conveniently after gym practice) to the little kids in his house. For spelling, Stick makes me practise word lists he gets off the Beating Dyslexia site, reading them over the phone and getting me to spell them back. That's embarrassing. I mean, some of the words I screw up are pretty simple. But, it isn't as embarrassing as phonics.

Stick bought me a *Barbie Does Phonics* book with a bright-pink cover and a smiling plastic girl. "Just think of Barbie's boobs," Stick advised as he handed it to me. Thank God Carly hasn't discovered it. As soon as I finish the stupid thing, I'm burning it.

Carly's been helping too. She asked if I wanted her to do my Social Studies essay. In the past I would have said yes. In fact, I would have been the one begging her, even paying her, to do it. But Stick reminded me that parkour is about overcoming obstacles quickly and efficiently, without disruption to your intended path. He said, when I got Carly to do my essays, when I lied, or sold my Ritalin — I only increased my obstacles. Made them harder to get over. And, now, looking back on it, I agree. That's why Stick told the truth about breaking into the brewery. Telling the truth was the most efficient way of solving that situation.

So, instead of saying yes to Carly's offer, I asked her to teach me how to write an essay. Surprisingly, Carly's a pretty good teacher. She broke down the five major kinds of essays into simple to follow steps. I didn't even know there *were* five kinds of essays. Now, for the first time in my life, I understand what's going on in class. For the first time *ever*, I don't feel stupid. I even scored not one but two marks over seventy.

Rocketing from my locker to Social Studies, I slide into my desk as the bell rings. Perfectly on time. I'm pretty happy. Today our essays come back, and I can see if all this effort is paying off. It's refreshing to be excited, instead of sick to my stomach.

The teacher starts by talking about world citizenship, the unit we've been working on. "Who read the material last night?"

I raise my hand. It's a first. But, not only did I read it, I also understood it. The article was about the Canadian Harambee Education Society, a society that gives scholarships to girls in Kenya and Tanzania. I even looked it up on YouTube.

"Martin." The teacher points at me, looking pleased. "What did you think of it?"

"I thought that the African saying they were using as a reason to only give scholarships to girls was a bit simple and sexist," I reply, my face growing hot and my voice wobbling. I've never really answered like this before; it's kind of freaky.

"So, you don't agree with the statement that if you educate a man, you educate an individual, but if you educate a woman, you educate a family?"

"Not entirely," I answer. "I think guys can educate others too." Stick could educate the whole world, as long the topic could relate to parkour.

The teacher nods and points to the girl

behind me, who adds her own opinion. The discussion is so much more clear when I actually know what everyone is talking about. In fact, I think Social Studies is getting to be my favourite subject.

A half-hour later the teacher hands back our essays. She pats my shoulder as she puts mine on the desk. "Good job, Martin. I'm really happy."

I sit there stunned, staring at my mark. Eighty-three per cent. *Holy crap!*

I'm pulled out of my trance when my name blares over the intercom, along with the words *Come to the office.*

What did I do now?

21

SERIOUSLY, WHAT DID I DO?

Essay inserted in my binder and binder tucked into my backpack. I walk to the office. I'm wracking my brain. I've been too busy to get into trouble lately, unless York finally spilled about the Ritalin. He was pretty pissed when I told him I wasn't selling it anymore. It's even worse when the secretary ushers me in and both my parents are sitting in front of the principal — all eyes turning on me.

Seriously, what did I do?

"Have a seat, Martin." The principal directs me to a chair by my dad. I sit, but try to subtly slide the chair away. It squeaks on the floor.

So much for subtle.

The principal clears his throat. "Martin, your marks have improved rather dramatically."

"Yeah," I say, drawing the word out. I'm not sure if he's taking this as a good thing or bad thing.

"We are concerned —" the principal continues.

"We think you're cheating," Dad bursts. "How are you suddenly getting marks ten or even twenty per cent higher than all your marks this year?"

"Try thirty." I pull out my essay, and hand it to my dad, grinning big.

"Did your sister write this for you?" Dad asks.

My grin fades. "No. I did it myself. I did all this myself."

"But," Mom says, "how are you doing it? It doesn't make sense."

"Easy. I've figured out I'm dyslexic."

"You're what?" Dad asks.

"Dyslexic. I have all the symptoms. Words move around on the page. Sometimes the page will even change colour under the word. Weird, huh? I always thought everyone saw that, but, as of three weeks ago, I've found out they don't."

"What are you talking about?" Dad growls. "I've looked online, that's never come up."

"Wrong search words?" I guess.

"This is bull —" Dad says.

"We do have other students with it." The principal interrupts him, then looks at me. "What makes you think you have dyslexia, Martin?"

"I did an online test, looked at some videos. They were all describing, well, me. I've had it my whole life. I mean, I remember having trouble way back in —"

"So, how do we fix it?" Dad growls. "Is there some kind of medication?"

"No, Dad. It's not something that can be cured like that. But, I can learn to control it."

"How?" Mom asks, her concern turning to interest. "What have you been doing?"

"Practising my reading and spelling.

Changing how I study. Working really hard."

"I can see that," the principal nods. "Good for you taking the initiative." He turns to my parents. "If what Martin suspects is true, the school can get funding to assist with his classes once he has been properly diagnosed."

Dad shakes his head. "That's fine. Martin is already registered in a program that will help him. He starts in the fall."

I freeze. My smile fades. "But, we made a deal. Seventy per cent on all my final exams, and I don't have to go. I'm going to get those marks."

"The deal is off," Dad returns. "If you really have this dyslexia, then military school is where you need to be."

My chest tightens. Lips go numb. Sweat rises. My cold shock is replaced by burning anger. I'm surprised I don't catch fire. I stand. Glare. Run out of the room, down the hall, and through the school doors. I run until I can't run any more. Until the burning in my gut retreats to a smoky smoulder, and I stop seeing everything in red.

22

I'M NOT STUPID!

"You skipped school?" Stick asks.

I'm sitting in his room, still angry. He discovered me seething on his front step when he arrived home.

"Yeah. All this work, all the good marks, and it didn't matter." I punch the bed. I would rather punch my dad in the head. "It was all just a big waste of time."

"Depends," Stick says.

"What depends?" I snap.

"Well, who you were working for? You or your dad?"

"Does it matter?"

"In parkour —"

"Screw parkour," I interrupt, not wanting another of Master Stick's lectures.

"In parkour," Stick continues, ignoring me, "you have to push yourself to *your* limits, to realize *your* dreams, go with *your* flow — not someone else's. So, who were you working for?"

"Me!" I get up and start pacing. "I'm tired of people calling me stupid. I'm not stupid. And I'm not lazy. I have to work ten times harder than everyone else to just come up even. And no one gets that!"

"So . . ." Stick leads.

"It's an obstacle," I say, getting where he's going.

Stick nods at me, a grin forming on his face urging me to go on.

"An obstacle I have to overcome directly and efficiently. Right?"

"Yeah," Stick says. "So, what are you going to do?"

"I going to go home, steal my camera and

my lenses back, sell enough of them to sign up for a whole summer of film school, and when the summer is over, I'll move to Vancouver and live on the streets until I find a way to get into the movie industry."

Stick's grin fades. "No. That's not right."

"So, what? It's easy."

"Life on the Vancouver streets, trying to break into an industry with almost no training is not easy." Stick scowls. "You're going to need university at the very least."

"I can't do university."

"Keep up with your practice and you can," Stick says. He looks at his hands, twisting his fingers in his fist. "Listen, all my parents care about is their crack pipes and needles. You're parents are tying themselves into knots trying to figure out how to help you. And, yeah, I get it, your dad is a dick. He's a liar. He's an ass-hole. But, don't write him off yet. Think about his real motives. He wants you to succeed."

I frown. "He wants to send me away."

"So, tell him what you want."

"How?" I spit.

"Did your dad even see your movie?"

I clamp my lips shut. Say nothing.

"Well?"

"I haven't shown him anything since I was eight."

"So, he doesn't know how amazing you are?"

"He doesn't know anything!" I shout. "He doesn't believe in dyslexia because it didn't pop up in his search engine when he used the words *stupid failure*. He says my movie-making is a big distraction. And he thinks this military school is going to be the ultimate solution to everything."

"So, educate him," Stick says. "Tell him who you are. Show him your film."

I don't say anything. Just stand there, smouldering.

"Remember when we were up on top of that sign?" Stick asks. "Make him feel that."

"I don't want to." Frustration stings my eyes and makes it hard to take a full breath.

"Don't want to or . . ." Stick asks, voice soft.

"I don't know how!" I grab my backpack off the floor and shoulder it. Open the bedroom door.

"Wait!" Stick calls.

I stop. Turn around. "What?"

"Where are you going?"

"Home."

Stick keeps a steady gaze. "Are you going to talk to your dad?"

"That depends."

"On what?" Stick asks.

I narrow my eyes, jaw stiff. "If he gives my camera back."

23

ARGUMENT PARKOUR

Mom's at the kitchen table when I walk in the door. Dad's with her.

"Martin. Come here," Dad commands.

"Give me back my camera first," I return, not moving from the doorway.

"Come here, and we'll talk about it," Mom cajoles, her long hair framing the concern on her face.

"No. Dad made a deal."

Dad clears his throat. "Let's discuss it."

His words blow oxygen on my already smouldering temper. "You said I could have my camera back if my marks went up.

They're up. Give it back."

Mom shoots him a look.

"Fine." He stands. "But at least talk with your mother."

I sit down, glaring. The table is covered with old report cards, elementary school assignments, and a couple of class pictures. Mom's been digging through her memory box. Dad's tablet is open to a dyslexia site.

So, they've been looking into it. Good.

Mom reaches across the table and lays her hand over mine. "I want to tell you that we believe you and we're sorry you had to figure this out on your own."

Dad returns, handing me my camera bags, saying, "And that's why you need a structured environment with small classes. It will —"

"We're done." I push my chair back.

"Martin, stop!" Mom gives Dad the evil eye. "We all know what your dad wants," she says. "But, we're not sure what you want."

"Are you going to listen?" I ask. "Or are you going to pretend to listen, make promises, then go back on your word?" I dare Dad to call me out.

He huffs. "Go ahead."

One hurdle down. It's like argument parkour. "I want to go to film school this summer."

Dad scrunches up his face, like he's smelled something bad.

"Dad, it's what I do! What I'm good at!"

"You're good at something?" Dad says, off the cuff. Mom kicks him under the table. I'm pretty sure, anyway. He lets out a low "oof" and immediately looks regretful.

"Dyslexia isn't only a disability," I explain. "It means that I see the world differently. It gives me an edge."

"That's a great way of looking at it," Mom says.

Dad just smiles. It doesn't look genuine. More like he's trying not to get kicked again.

I keep moving forward, just like Stick says. "There are lots of famous people who have dyslexia."

"Really?" Dad says sceptically.

"Steven Spielberg, Keira Knightley, and Orlando Bloom," I list.

"Oh, I like that Orlando Bloom," Mom says. "He's so cute."

Now it's Dad's turn to scowl at Mom.

"There are some athletes too," I go on. "Jackie Stewart, race car driver. Nolan Ryan, pitcher for the Texas Rangers. Steve Redgrave, who won Olympic gold in rowing five consecutive times." If anything is going to sell Dad on the fact that dyslexia doesn't mean you're stupid, it will be through sports. Luckily I memorized some names on the way home, just in case.

Dad whistles. "I didn't know."

I lean forward, precision jumping point to point. "This problem doesn't have to define me. Now that I know what I'm dealing with, I need a bit of time to adjust to the fact that I'm not stupid, I'm dyslexic."

"Yes. I understand that, Martin," Dad says. "And that's why the military school will help —"

"But it won't!" I yell. "That school is for kids with ADHD —"

"And other learning disabilities," Dad soothes.

"Yeah, like oppositional defiant disorder," I counter. "But I don't have that either, *by the way*. I've seen the school's site and, okay, they might have some dyslexic kids, but it's not really what they're about." I look into my dad's eyes. It's like leaping up to a high wall. I put all my energy into this one point. Try to get him to finally understand. "Dad, I know I need help, but I need the right kind of help."

Dad blinks. "All I've ever wanted was to help you."

I think of all those times he has called me stupid, lazy, a loser. "Sometimes," I say, "it doesn't feel like it."

"I'm sorry," Dad says. "Really. I just didn't understand your problem."

"*We* didn't understand," Mom amends.

"So, can I do anything?" Dad asks. His face flushes. He's getting frustrated. "How about a tutor? One who specializes in this dyslexia?"

"Yeah. A tutor." I nod encouragingly. "That would be excellent." Dad is finally getting it. I can't believe it.

"I still want you to go to university," Dad says.

I nod. "I'll probably have to at least go to film school if I want to be a Hollywood director."

Dad scoffs. "I doubt they let Lego film-makers apply."

"You would be surprised," I mutter under my breath. I reach across the table for his tablet and pull up the contest, clicking on my film in the runners-up section before passing it back to him. "Look. This is what I do."

Mom and Dad watch the images flicker past. Stick and his crew, the bottle, the moon. My words coming out of the speaker:

Stupid. Maybe I am stupid. It's what everyone calls me. Stupid. Loser. Dumb. Lazy. And the labels, they seem so real. Especially when words spin, drift, blur. Sometimes I get lost. Daydreaming. Forget to check where I'm walking. Like I could travel for days in a haze of imagination. The glow of a bottle in the floodlight can hold me captivated for seconds, minutes, hours. Is it stupid? Am I? Probably. But, I see things you don't. I see my city in ways your normal brain can't imagine. And my spinning, upside-down world can express my dreams while you sit there, stagnant, watching the sports channel. Turning to stone. Letting your life drain away. Jealous of my creativity. So, while I might be stupid, I'm not dumb, or a loser, or lazy. I'm creative. Unique. An artist. And this is my world.

The final image of Stick on top of the sign makes him look for all the world like a superhero overseeing his city. Pride surges through me. It's a great shot. It's a great movie. Stick is right; it should have won.

I look at my parents, wondering what their reactions will be. Wait for Dad to mock me or be mad for calling him out. At the very least, say I'm a loser, like the judges basically did.

But, while Mom is crying, Dad is . . . smiling? *Really?*

He has this huge, proud grin on his face that I only see when he looks at Carly.

"Wow," he says. "You've come a long way from Lego. You should have said something."

"I guess I was being *stupid*." It comes out quick. One more jab.

Dad's face turns pink. He gets the message.

Dad and I, we both have habits. They're not going to change overnight. I know what Stick would say about that. Parkour is about practice and patience and starting with the basics. It's about repetition, hard work, and finding your own path. He would tell me to keep trying, that things will happen. I almost laugh thinking how deep Stick's philosophy has wormed into my mind.

"That film of yours should have won," Dad says. "When's the next contest?"

I shrug. "I haven't looked for one. I mean, I lost. Besides, I have problems reading the